ACROSS THE NARROW SEAS

In the vast armada assembled for the D-Day invasion was a small coaster, the *S.S. Radgate*. In charge of her guns was Sergeant Fred Mason of the Maritime Royal Artillery, and through his eyes we see the blood, agony and confusion of D-Day, and London under the flying bombs. Against the tension of the ever-present threat of mines, bombs and shells, the story switches from London to the Normandy beaches, to Mulberry harbour, storms and tragedy.

Books by James Pattinson
in the Ulverscroft Large Print Series:

THE WHEEL OF FORTUNE

JAMES PATTINSON

ACROSS THE NARROW SEAS

Complete and Unabridged

ULVERSCROFT
Leicester

First published in Great Britain

First Large Print Edition
published February 1993

British Library CIP Data

Pattinson, James
    Across the narrow seas.—Large print ed.—
Ulverscroft large print series: general fiction
I. Title
823.914 [F]

ISBN 0–7089–2811–0

Published by
F. A. Thorpe (Publishing) Ltd.
Anstey, Leicestershire
Set by Words & Graphics Ltd.
Anstey, Leicestershire
Printed and bound in Great Britain by
T. J. Press (Padstow) Ltd., Padstow, Cornwall

1

'Radgate'

THE sun was pushing its rays of heat through the morning veil of smoke and vapour that hung over London as they went up-river. Shadows of cranes and ships' masts trembled on the water. A tug hooted like a street urchin — three jeering hoots escaping with a white rag of steam. The engine of the launch vibrated, and Mason could smell the hot odour of petrol and lubricating oil that came from it.

"Going to be a hot day," Sergeant Walters said.

Mason grunted. He was not so much interested in the weather as in finding his ship — the coaster S.S. *Radgate*. He should have embarked the previous day; the Army lorry that had brought him down from Woodford with three other lance-sergeants had nosed its way into a dozen wharves where the *Radgate* might have been hiding without finding so much as a scent of the ship. It was like a phantom that had vanished with the night.

Green and Sanderson and McLaverty had been luckier; they had found their berths — all little coasters of between 500 and 800 tons. Mason had helped them with their kit, had watched them climbing their various gang-planks, and had waved a hand in farewell. He had lived with them for three weeks, had shared a mess with them, drunk beer with them in the evenings — too much beer, maybe — paraded with them, played cards with them; now with a wave of the hand they were gone, and as likely as not he would never see any of them again. And if he did not there would be no regrets. Men came and went; they passed by you in an endless stream — men from Liverpool, Glasgow, Birmingham, Newcastle, Nottingham, Exeter, from Inverness, Belfast, and Dublin, from the Isle of Man and the Hebrides, all drifting into your line of vision and drifting on, forgotten, maybe killed; you could never keep track of them all; you could not feel the loss of all of them.

So Green and Sanderson and McLaverty had gone, climbing aboard their allotted ships to settle down in new, strange quarters, to adjust themselves to those quarters and make of them for a while something that would pass for home, finding therein what comfort they could. They had gone: Green to an old collier that had been bringing coal from the Tyne to Battersea for so many years one might have supposed it had worn a pathway through the sea, that the very iron of its hull could recognize each cliff, each buoy, each lighthouse on the entire length of that coastline from Shields to Southend pier, so that, like a horse grown used to the repetition of one journey, it could find its own way with no need for a man's hand to guide it. Sanderson had gone to a ship whose sides were so bespattered with squares and rectangles of red lead paint on the drab background of grey that they had the appearance of a patchwork quilt, and McLaverty, luckiest of all, to a smart Dutch motor-vessel shining with new paint and polished brass, a captain's pride, with everything

3

in place, everything in order.

But there had been no ship for Mason, only scratching of heads and attempts to be helpful: "The *Radgate*? Ah, she was 'ere, but she left. No, can't really say where she went to. Up-river, likely. Mebbe Rotherhithe or Wapping."

It was all vague. In the maze of London's dockland you could search for a ship for a year and never find it. When it was too late to hunt any longer the lorry went back to Woodford, Mason in a snarling mood at the prospect of unpacking kit and settling down in the billet for one more night.

It was during breakfast that Sergeant Walters had said: "Shouldn't you have joined the *Radgate* yesterday? Thought you went off with McLaverty and that crowd."

"I came back," Mason said. "The *Radgate* has gone into hiding. We couldn't find the damned tub anywhere. I suppose it does exist?"

"No doubt about it. She moved up-river. These little coasters are apt to shift about. They're all loaded, you see — have been for months, some of 'em, just waiting for the balloon to go up. Job is to find moorings for them all; the river's cluttered, choked with 'em. But I know where the *Radgate* is. You come with me. I've got a few jobs to do, inspections and what not, and there's a launch laid on. I can put you aboard."

"Suits me," Mason said. "I'm fed up with this place. What's the ship carrying?"

"Nice cargo. High explosive."

The launch was moving up-river against the flow of water coming down with the ebb-tide — grey, filthy water, dropping away from the shining mud on either bank, water swirling down through Limehouse Reach and past the West India Dock pier, the flotsam of the city bobbing and dancing on its surface. A string of barges went past at the tail of a tug, and the launch butted into the slanting waves of their wash. Water slapped against its bows, sending bursts of spray over into the cockpit where the soldiers were standing. The engine coughed, seemed to hesitate for a moment as though doubtful of its own strength, then picked up again.

The R.A.S.C. corporal at the helm addressed the engine without rancour: "Come on, you bastard!"

"What's wrong with it?" Mason asked.

"Bastard petrol; no damn good these days. God knows what they put in it." The engine stammered again, and the corporal cajoled it in a sad weary voice: "Now, now, old girl; don't make trouble. Not at the beginning of the day. Give us a chance."

They were coming round the bend of the river, skirting that peninsula in which were hidden the intricacies of the Surrey Commercial docks, the docks with the fine-sounding names like Russia and Quebec, Greenland and Lavender and Lady. The sun was stoking up, beginning to burn; Mason could feel it on the skin of his dark, bony face.

"You been in coasters before?" Walters asked.

Mason shook his head. "Not me. Deep-sea every time."

"What ship were you in last?"

"*Mauretania* — ten months — South Africa, Colombo, Port Tewfik; then the Atlantic ferry racket — strap-hanging

6

Yanks across from New York and Halifax."

Walters grinned. "*Mauretania*, eh? You'll find a difference. The *Radgate* is eight hundred tons; that's a bit of a come-down from thirty-four thousand."

"I'll get used to it," Mason said.

You got used to anything in time; and not so much time either. You got used to discomfort and broken sleep and rough food, to the sick flutter in the stomach that was fear. It was all part of the business of war, in which you became no longer an individual but a number dressed in khaki. It was the number that came first, then your rank, then your surname, last of all your initials. So here he was with a number close to the one and a half million mark and the rank of lance-sergeant. Mason, Peter Roger; age, twenty-eight; height, six feet and half an inch; weight, thirteen stone five pounds; beaked nose, thin mouth, and jet-black hair. Peter Mason, once farmer, then soldier, now half soldier half sailor.

"Tinker, tailor, soldier, sailor — "

"But not rich man," Walters said, with

a laugh. "Not on our pay. Not if the War lasts through another winter. When things get going they'll move fast."

The R.A.S.C. corporal spat with fine precision over the gunwale of the launch. "That's what you think. But suppose this invasion turns out to be a ruddy failure. We had a go once before — at Dieppe. Remember? Suppose Jerry pushes the whole flaming lot, guns and lorries and tanks and men, back into the flaming sea. What then?"

"Dieppe was only a raid. This time it's the showdown, the finish."

"I hope you're right. I've got a job to get back to."

On either side of the river the coasters huddled, their hatches battened down. Every pier, every jetty, every mooring seemed to have its quota. Mason had never seen so many little ships. Half the coastal traffic of Britain must have come to a standstill while these ships were held and loaded, waiting for the day.

"What a target if he came over with a few hundred heavy bombers, a few Junkers 188's! What an almighty flame-up that'd be!"

"But he won't," Walters said. "He hasn't got the planes to do it."

Over the vast, sprawling city the barrage-balloons hovered motionless, shining, fat and silver, in the sun, as though it were they that supported London with their cables and not London that held them prisoners. Guards and prisoners too, swollen with the idea of their own importance; monstrous silver whales floating in a pale blue sea. Mason wondered how many planes they had brought down, how many possible attacks they had discouraged during these past five years. Perhaps no one would ever know.

The R.A.S.C. flag of the launch fluttered from its tiny jack-staff; astern the water foamed and bubbled under the churning screw; waves slanted back from the bows, fanning out on either side to form a wide arrow pointing the way upriver. They came round the curve, and ahead lay Rotherhithe on the one side and Wapping on the other. Walters scanned the Rotherhithe bank, screwing up his eyes against the glare of the sun. With his smooth, round, hairless face, he looked strangely child-like.

"She's moved again," he said. He pointed to a cluster of ships. "She was with that lot; but she's gone."

Mason nodded — resigned, cynical. This was the sort of thing he had become used to in five years of war. Events never turned out as expected; things were never where they should have been. And you had so little power of control. This ship, now: somebody had decided that he should join it; he had had no voice in the matter; he had been sent to where the ship ought to have been, and it had gone. However much he might have exerted himself, he could not have prevented that from happening. He remembered times when it had happened before: once he had been ordered to join a ship that was supposed to be moving into the Canada dock in Liverpool. When he arrived the ship was not there; it had never been there; it was in fact already in a convoy outward bound for Canada — the country, not the dock. An error by some clerk, a misunderstood telephone message, had perhaps saved his life; for that ship had been torpedoed and sunk in mid Atlantic. On such slender threads did a man's existence depend.

"We'd better go on a bit," Walters said. "And keep an eye open."

"Your eye," Mason said. "I don't know what the *Radgate* looks like."

"You will before you've finished with her."

"No doubt."

"Don't mind me," the R.A.S.C. corporal said sarcastically. "I got all day. Free trips up and down the river. It's all part of the service. Maybe you'd like to go to Kew gardens or Hampton Court. Just say the word."

"There's a bright boy," Walters said. "You keep your mind on your work, else you'll be running into a bloody barge or something."

"What do you take me for?"

"Don't ask me. You mightn't like the answer."

The launch went up-river slowly, with Sergeant Walters scanning the motionless ships on either side. The corporal belched suddenly and violently.

"Maybe she's slipped into one of the

docks. You'd need X-ray eyes to see her then."

"Why should she do that? She's got her cargo."

"How should I know? I'm not the brains of the outfit."

"Thank God for that," Walters said.

They came up through the Pool towards Tower Bridge, the grey and white battlements of the Tower away on their right. The sound of the launch's engine came echoing back as they went under the arch, reflected from the brick walls on either side and the iron roadway above. The water was rippling past the piers of the bridge, lapping at them eagerly, as though what had stood for centuries might even now be finally pushed aside and beaten down, the permanent made impermanent, the solid churned into mud.

They came through the bridge, keeping near the middle of the stream. Walters gave a cry of triumph and slapped his leg.

"Okay. There she is — on your port side."

The corporal followed with his eyes

the direction of Walters' pointing finger. "That one?"

"That's the baby."

The *Radgate* was moored by Hay's Wharf alongside two other coasters which formed stepping-stones between her and the shore. She was a little grey ship with a well-deck forward of the bridge and a raised quarter-deck, straight bows, and rubbing-strakes along each side. From the poop rose a cluster of deck-housing, ventilator-shafts like outsize ear-trumpets, and lifeboats slung on old-fashioned, swan-necked davits. From this cluster sprouted a single tall, thin funnel, soot-blackened at the tip and standing up very straight and stern like the grimy, admonishing finger of some itinerant preacher. A line of washing hung from the derrick boom across the forward hatch, limp and motionless in the still, warm air of the morning; and on a board tied to the side of the bridge was painted in white letters the name *Radgate*.

"Your ship, sir," Walters said, with a trace of mockery in his voice. "Not perhaps quite up to *Mauretania* standards, but the best we can do at short notice."

13

Mason did not trouble to answer. He was looking with a practised eye at what was visible of the armament. The guns were covered, but he could tell from the shape and size of the canvas covers exactly what they concealed. On each wing of the bridge a 20-millimetre Oerlikon pointed its long barrel to the sky, looking in its grey canvas hood rather like a badly rolled umbrella — one of the genuine Mrs Gamp variety. Above the deckhouse on the poop another circular gun platform protected by a steel wall could be discerned, and from it another, rather larger canvas thrust its apex skyward. A twin. Two single Oerlikons and one double: it was not bad armament for a ship of only 800 tons. No twelve-pounder or four-inch, of course; but there was not likely to be much use for such guns on this job. Somebody had got to blast a way through the Atlantic Wall, but that was not a job for the *Radgate*. She simply had to carry supplies, and try not to get blown out of the water in doing so.

Two seamen were hosing down the coaster's decks as the launch drew alongside, and the unmistakable odour of wet iron and timber steaming in the sun caught at Mason's nostrils. It was two months since he had last been at sea — two months of training, of refresher courses, during which time he had not set foot on the deck of a sea-going ship. He was glad to be back on the job; he preferred being in a ship to being on shore. Two months was enough — too much. Foot-drill, gun-drill, aircraft recognition, firing practice, and lectures, lectures, lectures: he was sick of it all. Perhaps when this last big push was over there would be a quick finish. It had been long enough.

Yet supposing, just supposing the invasion should be a flop; supposing it turned out as the corporal had suggested and the invading forces were thrown back into the sea. What then? But they would not be. He was sure of it. This time there would be no retreat. This time it was going to be the pay-off.

Mason remembered the bitterness of Dunkirk; he remembered the retreat to the coast, fighting all the way; he remembered the days and nights on the beaches waiting for the little ships.

Dunkirk had been a miracle, but no amount of wishful thinking could make it into anything but a defeat. They had been driven out of France, kicked out. And lucky to get out at all, lucky to save their skins, leaving the great mass of their precious equipment behind. You could not call that a victory.

But now the tables had turned. In a few more weeks, perhaps only a few more days, they would be going back to wipe out for ever the bitterness of Dunkirk and all those other defeats. But he would not be going ashore. Three years ago he had exchanged the land for the sea, had become a soldier-sailor to man the guns of merchant vessels sailing to America, to South Africa, and to Russia on the long, cold, bitter haul across the bloodstained Arctic Ocean.

He had never regretted the change — until now. Now he would have liked to be going back on to French soil, to wipe out his own personal memory of Dunkirk. And then he told himself that he was a fool. As if he had not had enough of fighting! As if anyone in his senses would want to push himself near the firing-line! Let somebody else do that — somebody who was looking for glory. He wanted to come out of this nonsense with a whole skin; he had had some punctures in it already; he could manage very nicely without any more.

The launch bumped against the side of the ship. A soldier who had been morosely silent and inactive until this moment flung a painter over the bulwark and a man in greasy dungarees and a cloth cap made the end fast.

"What's the trouble now?" he asked.

He was a thick, rather short man, powerful-looking, massive-shouldered, with strong, sunburnt hands on the backs of which grew a black mat of hair like the tattered remains of woollen mittens. His face would have delighted a cartoonist, it had so many kinks and twists that should never have been there — a fold at the bridge of the nose that might have been the result of a blow early in life, a scar that lifted one side of his lip in a perpetual sneer, grooves and pockmarks innumerable. His nose was bulbous, his chin thrust forward belligerently, and his eyes very bright, quick-moving, intelligent. The skin of the face was the colour of old brown paint, and had some of the same hard, dry surface texture. It was a face that looked as though it had been weathered and salted, weathered and salted, until it had become as impervious to the sea and the elements as the carved figurehead of an old sailing-ship.

His voice was harsh. It was as if a crow had learned to speak. "You coming aboard, then?"

Walters clambered on to the cabin-roof of the launch; from there he could reach the ship's bulwark. He climbed on board, Mason followed him.

"Is the captain anywhere about?" Walters asked.

The man in the dungarees and the cloth cap nodded. "He is."

"Can you take me to him?"

"No need, sergeant. You're looking at him. Captain Garner — that's me. Now, what would you be wanting?"

Walters showed no surprise. He had had plenty of experience with coasters; he knew that their captains were not inclined to worry so much about gold braid and polish as the masters of ocean-going ships. To Mason it was more of a shock. From the remote, god-like being who had commanded the great liner from which he had come this was a change indeed. But he kept his thoughts to himself. His face showed no emotion.

"You're having a change of crew," Walters said. "One sergeant to replace one bombardier. All right?"

Captain Garner allowed his keen glance to rest for a moment on Sergeant Mason; then he looked back again at Walters.

"I've no fault to find with Bombardier Betts. Why do you have to take him away?" He seemed to resent this change. Perhaps he had got used to Betts, and had no desire to take on a new man. "You people are always coming and going. Why don't you get things settled?"

"Doesn't do gunners any good to stay too long in one ship. They get slack, need shaking up. But that's not the reason why we're taking Betts. It's orders from higher up — got to have a senior N.C.O. as gun layer on this game."

Captain Garner rubbed his chin, and the hard stubble rasped under his fingers.

19

"Okay then. What must be, must be. But I'll be sorry to lose the bombardier."

"I'm glad to hear it," Walters said.

Garner said: "You'd better come along to my cabin. You've got papers and suchlike, I've no doubt. Too many damned papers these days — forms for everything. Get rid of the forms and things would run a sight smoother — that's my opinion."

Relieving himself thus of his resentment against the formalities of Government service, he led them up a short ladder to the midships accommodation and through a door-way into a small cabin fitted with a single bunk, a settee, and a writing-table. Curled up under the table was a big Alsatian dog which raised its head when the men entered and eyed them warily.

"All right, Cerberus," Garner said. "You go to sleep again." He put his foot on the dog's head and pushed it down. The dog obediently rested his head on its legs again, but kept his eyes open, not taking chances.

Garner eased himself into a chair and began to fill the capacious bowl of a black, short-stemmed pipe, ramming the tobacco down with his stubby thumb.

"You take the dog to sea?" Walters asked.

"Always. He's a good seaman — better than many I've known that went about on two legs and called themselves sailors. And in port you couldn't ask for a better watchman."

"What happened to his other heads?" Mason asked.

Garner shot a keen glance at him, as though surprised to discover any knowledge of classical mythology in an Army sergeant.

"This one isn't guarding Hades — nor even a hell-ship. He only needs one head."

Mason laughed. "I'm glad to hear it."

Walters pulled out a wad of forms and began sorting through them. Mason noticed a violin-case lying on the bunk.

"You play the fiddle, captain?"

Garner jerked his head in a nod which gave the impression that the head was mounted on a stout coiled spring; it dipped forward, then went back and vibrated a little before settling into its normal position. "I played in the streets once. There was a depression. Maybe you don't remember that. They didn't want seamen then."

"I remember," Walters said. "I'm not so young. I had a job in a shipping office — three-ten a week and scared out of my wits of getting the sack. We don't want that again."

"It'll come," Garner said gloomily. "You bet your life it'll come when this lot's over."

The smoke rose from his pipe, wrapping his head in a grey cloud and blurring the rough outline. A captain in dungarees and a cloth cap. Mason thought; a captain who had played the fiddle in the streets to keep himself from starving, and took with him to sea an Alastian dog named Cerberus. He wondered how old the man was, and decided that a face like that was not one to give away the secret of age.

He left Garner and Walters talking together and went to see about getting his kit on board. He found that the job had already been done, and that the kit bags were lying on the tarpaulin cover

22

of the forward hatch. A bombardier was leaning on the bulwarks talking to the launch crew. His glasses made him look studious.

"You Bombardier Betts?" Mason asked.

The man straightened up. "That's me, sergeant. You're taking my place, I hear. Would you like to see your quarters?" He grinned as he asked the question, and Mason wondered what was amusing him. "I'll give you a hand up with your kit."

He took one of the bags and Mason followed with another. Betts led the way up two flights of steps to the navigating-bridge, went into the wheelhouse and through a doorway into the chart-room. He dumped the kitbag he had been carrying.

"This is where you doss, sergeant."

"This?"

The room was narrow, rectangular in shape. A square window looked out towards the after part of the ship, and under the window, fixed to the wall, was a settee. Opposite the settee, and divided from it by only a few feet of floor-space, was the chart-table, fitted with drawers, and having at one end

23

a nest of pigeon-holes for the stowage of signal flags. A wireless set, signalling lamps, rockets, emergency flares, and various other bits and pieces of gear cluttered the room. There seemed to be no order, nor great cleanliness; the floor was grimy, brasswork tarnished; on the chart-table were a number of blotches that looked like candlegrease. Notches serrating the edge of the table might have been cut to register some account, or, more likely, might have been the work of an idle youth armed with a clasp-knife and time to waste. Half a dog biscuit lay in one corner.

As Mason's glance travelled round the room Betts stood looking at him with amused interest.

"Proper quarters are full up, you see. Coasters don't usually take such a load of gunners. There's two naval ratings manning the twin Oerlikon — they've got a cabin down aft. Then there's three Army gunners — two of them share a cabin in the fo'c'sle and one has to muck in with the crew. That leaves no spare bunk for the detachment commander, so he has to doss in here."

"That's all very fine," Mason said, "but what happens when the ship's at sea? This room will be in use all the time."

Betts shrugged. "That's your worry now. Since I came on board we haven't been out of the river. Maybe they think you'll be on watch all the time — won't want any sleep."

"Maybe," Mason said grimly. He did not like the arrangement. The chart-room had never been meant for use as a cabin. There was nowhere to lay out his things; he would have to keep everything stowed in the kitbags; and no doubt people would be for ever moving in and out of the room. It was a rotten arrangement. He looked at the settee. It was upholstered in a grey-blue cloth, rather worn, with the horsehair stuffing bursting out from one end. It was this which was to be his bed. He tested it with his fingers. A pretty hard bed.

"What are all those hairs?" he asked.

"Cerberus uses it when he feels like taking a nap."

"That damned Alsatian? What if he takes a fancy to the settee when you want to get your head down?"

"You have to be tactful," Betts said. "Cerberus is all right if you don't upset him, but you want to keep on his right side; he could turn nasty."

"I'll bet he could. Any fleas?"

"Just a few, perhaps. But he usually takes them with him. I think he's attached to them."

"So long as they're attached to him," Mason said. "Hell! Why did the Old Man have to bring a dog that size into a ship as small as this? Why couldn't he have been content with a cat?"

"There's a cat too," Betts said.

★ ★ ★

Betts left the ship with Sergeant Walters in the launch. He did not appear at all sorry to go; perhaps he had had enough of the chart-room settee and Cerberus' fleas; perhaps he was simply resigned to any move that might be forced upon him. By leaving the *Radgate* he did at least stand the chance of being put on board a ship bound for America or Australia, and of missing the invasion. He might have preferred the known hazards of an Atlantic convoy to the unknown ones of running ammunition to the coast of France.

Mason rested his hands on the sun-warmed iron of the bulwark and watched the launch surging away from the ship's side. It moved out in a wide curve and headed downstream, the water creaming and bubbling from its propeller and leaving a gradually vanishing trail of foam on the dirty surface of the river. Sergeant Walters lifted a hand in farewell and Mason acknowledged it with a wave of his own hand. He had known Walters for less than a week, and Betts for no more than half an hour; he knew that it was quite possible that he would never see either of them again. He pushed himself away from the bulwark and went in search of his gunners.

2

Settling In

THE gunners were new to Mason. Sometimes you came across men with whom you had been to sea or had met at one of the detachments at home or abroad, and that made things easier. But he had never seen any of these ones before. He did not much care for the look of them, but he recognized the feeling of aversion for what it was — a part of his character. He did not mix easily with strangers; he liked to get to know a man thoroughly before thawing. He knew that some people thought him prickly, but the knowledge did not worry him. If he did not attract friends easily perhaps the ones he did gain were more worth the having.

As for these men, perhaps he would get on with them all right when he had become used to them, when their faces had become familiar, part of the background of his life. Nevertheless, there were some men with whom you could never get along — smart boys, sea-lawyers, men who were always ready to search out reasons why they should not obey the orders of their superiors. This fellow Scarr looked like one of that sort.

Gunner Scarr appeared to be about thirty. He was a little man with a wizened, pinched-up face that looked as though some one had grasped it in a very big hand and had squeezed it in upon itself. There was a sharpness about it, too — sharp nose, sharp chin, sharp eyes. A sharp customer altogether, Mason thought. He disliked Scarr at sight, and he did not believe that, however much he might see of him, he would ever get rid of that dislike. Rather was it probable that closer acquaintance would have the opposite effect. Perhaps it was this instinctive dislike that made his voice harsh, his expression bleak.

"When did you shave last?"

Scarr's right hand went up to his chin as if to test the growth of stubble. Perhaps he was wondering whether he could get away with a lie, the tale of a blunt razor-blade or cold shaving-water. But the beard was too thick for that; no man could have shaved that morning and grown so much facial hair in so short a time.

"Yesterday, sarge," he said.

"Why not today?"

The gunner screwed his face up into a smaller, even sharper-looking feature; he shuffled his plimsoll-shod feet on the iron deck and leaned his head on one side as if he were going to rest its black-haired weight on one shoulder. He was dressed in greasy denim trousers, frayed at the bottoms and held up by a length of cord knotted at the waist; his shirt was the usual Army type — khaki, collarless, open at the neck to reveal a growth of dark hair creeping up from Scarr's chest like a badly woven mat. Taken all in all, he was, Mason thought, as scruffy a soldier as you were likely to find. His voice was thin, with a whining, self-excusing quality.

"Well, you know how it is, sarge, on board of a ship like this — no hot water when you want it, no proper washin' arrangements at all, as you might say. Can't do everything according to the book — "

Mason cut in on him: "Go and get shaved now."

"Now, sarge?"

"You're not deaf, are you? That's what I said. And in future you'll shave every morning. Got it?"

"I got it, sarge." Scarr moved away and disappeared inside the forecastle. Mason turned to the other two gunners.

"Let's have your names. Then we'll know where we are."

They answered promptly. They had seen how this new N.C.O. had dealt with Scarr, and they were prepared to move warily.

"Rickman, sergeant."

"Gates, sergeant."

Rickman was a boy, smooth-cheeked, with blue eys and a mass of fair curly hair. A pretty boy, Mason thought cynically; maybe too pretty.

"How old are you, Rickman?"

The boy seemed to jerk upright, forcing his shoulders back as if afraid of revealing any lack of maturity.

"Nineteen, sergeant."

Mason did not ask how old the other man was. Gates looked middle-aged. His was a squat dumpling of a figure with its maximum circumference at the waist. His hair was greying, and he had a set of false teeth that looked rather too big for his mouth, so that it seemed as if he was for ever trying to stretch his lips over them, and as if when he forgot to do so the lips slipped back in a toothy grin. He looked good-tempered, cheerful.

"I want to have a look at the guns," Mason said. "Then at your quarters."

It was best to start as you meant to go on. Once let gunners get the idea that anything would do and you had the devil's own job smartening things up. Some men would work without the goad of discipline; others needed perpetually keeping up to the mark.

They climbed up to the bridge and crowded into the gunbox on the starboard wing. In it there was just room for a man to move round as he swivelled the gun — but no more.

"Get the cover off."

Rickman and Gates moved smartly to

carry out the order. Mason did not think he would have any trouble with these two; they were not the type. Scarr might be a different proposition. But he could deal with Scarr. He had had tougher boys than that to deal with.

The stiff canvas rustled as the cover was lifted off, and Mason examined the Oerlikon. Moisture had condensed on the grey-black metal; there were spots of rust here and there; the bore, which should in Mason's opinion have been gleaming like polished silver, was dull.

"When was this gun last cleaned?"

Richman looked at Gates, waiting for the older man to answer. Gates said hesitantly: "Yesterday, I think — "

"Don't give me that," Mason said sharply. "D'you think I haven't seen a gun before? This wasn't cleaned yesterday, nor the day before by the look of it."

"It was cleaned last week, sarge," Rickman said eagerly, trying to abate Mason's anger.

"Last week! What do you do with your time? Sit around on your behinds?" he looked at the Oerlikon with distaste. It

33

offended his sense of fitness to see a neglected gun. There was a saying in the Artillery: 'Clean gun, dirty billets; clean billets, dirty gun.' For his part he could never see any reason why either should be dirty.

"All right," he said. "Let's go and look at the others. I suppose they're about the same."

He realized that it wasn't these men who should be blamed, but the bombardier who had been in charge of them — Betts. You could not expect gunners to be smart under a slack N.C.O. Captain Garner had been satisfied with Betts, but that meant little. Ships' captains did not as a rule know much about guns, and were not in a position to judge the efficiency of a gunner. Betts might have made himself popular with Garner, but it was rapidly becoming evident to Mason that as an N.C.O. he had been less than efficient. Well, it was up to him to tighten things up. And he would see to that.

The port gun was, if anything, worse than the starboard one. Mason examined it in tight-lipped silence and then turned to Rickman. "You can start on this

34

straight away. Gates, you come with me. We'll take a look at the twin. Maybe it'll be twice as bad.

"The naval ratings look after that one," Gates said, disclaiming responsibility in advance. "It's just above their cabin, you see. Handy for manning."

"Where are the ratings?" Mason asked. "I haven't seen anything of them."

"Gone ashore to collect their pay. They should be back this afternoon."

"I'll have a look at their quarters when they come aboard, but we'll see the gun now."

He allowed Gates to lead the way down from the bridge and along the quarter-deck to the poop. Gates walked in a rolling style, his behind pressed tightly into the seat of his trousers. The sleeves of his shirt were rolled up above the elbow, and Mason, walking behind him, noticed a scar that stretched almost the whole length of the inner part of his right forearm. It had pulled the flesh up in a white ridge.

"Have you been wounded?" he asked.

Gates did not trouble to turn his head. He simply answered, as though it were a matter of no importance: "Yes. Torpedoed. Russia convoy. Ripped it on a bit of iron when I was sliding down the side of the ship. Not a wound really, not as you would call a wound. Just an accident. I ought to have been more careful."

He began to climb the ladder to the poop. Mason felt a little warmer towards him. Gates too had been on the Russia run; he had had his ship sunk under him in the Arctic Ocean, and that was no pleasant experience even without counting the sliced-up arm. Yet Gates himself was sure that it was not a genuine wound; he seemed, in fact, to be half ashamed of it, rating himself a fool for having been so careless as to scratch himself. Mason knew fellows who would have bragged about it, shot a line; but not this tubby little grey-haired man with the rolling walk who dismissed it with a few casual words. Gates did not look promising material, but he might be a useful man for all that.

The twin Oerlikon had a roomier platform than the bridge guns. Mounted above the poop deckhouse a little way aft of the funnel, it commanded a wide arc of fire, and the twin barrels were capable of pumping out a very useful stream of 20-millimetre anti-aircraft shells — very useful indeed. Mason could remember the time, a few years back, when many ocean-going merchantman would have been glad of just one such gun. But then they had had to make do with what they could get — obsolete Lewises, Marlins, and Hotchkisses, with here and there an unreliable Hispano.

They pulled the cover off the twin, and Mason was agreeably surprised to find that it was in first-rate order — clean, oiled, rustless, moving easily on its mounting. Mason hummed a snatch of tune in satisfaction. This was how he liked to see a gun. He loosened the wing-nuts on the ammunition locker and looked inside. Loaded magazines were neatly stacked.

"Navy seem to be on their toes, anyway," he said. "What are they — seamen-gunners?"

"One seaman-gunner and one gunlayer. The bombardier used to leave them pretty much to themselves. They look after this gun; we look after the other two."

It seemed to Mason that Betts had been altogether too easy-going. Admittedly you could not go in for too much spit and polish on board ships of this kind, but there was no excuse for allowing things to become slovenly. Slovenly gunners were bad gunners, and bad gunners too often became dead gunners. You had to keep up to the mark. It was wounding to his regimental pride to find that the only clean gun in the ship was that maintained by the naval ratings.

"Right," he said. "Get the cover on. Then I'll take a look at your quarters."

He looked across the river before descending from the gun platform. There was plenty of movement on its surface — launches, tugs, lighters, ships. Here was the dark thread meandering through the sprawling pattern of London — this river that had made the city, brought it wealth and power. Out of this grey, muddy stream the city had grown, a city that was at once Britain's strength and weakness, a city holding the country's destiny in the hollow of its iron hand, a city open to destruction from the air.

Mason wondered how it all worked, all this complicated coming and going, loading and unloading; this spider's web of roads and railways, this ant-heap of dwellings, this maze of docks and warehouses, offices and shops and factories; it was all so vast, so monstrous, so inhuman; it ought long since to have ground to a standstill, to have suffered extinction by reason of its very overgrowth. And yet it continued to tick; it had been pounded and battered and burned, and still it worked; it was a miracle past Mason's understanding. He put a leg over the steel wall of the gun platform and went backward down the iron ladder to the deck.

Scarr had cut himself in shaving, and he looked aggrieved, as though he blamed Mason for that cut, and felt that some compensation was due to him. Mason ordered him up to the bridge to help Rickman with the Oerlikons.

"And remember — I shall examine them afterwards. I want them clean — really clean. Understand?"

Scarr began to grumble. "All that soot

an' stuff. You can't keep guns clean." He dabbed at the cut with a handkerchief that looked capable of injecting blood-poison into his arteries. "Waste of time."

"Get moving," Mason said.

Scarr looked once into Mason's face and decided to do as he was told. He shuffled away towards the bridge, still dabbing at the cut, his loosely tied plimsolls slapping the deck like the flippers of a seal.

Gates led the way into the cabin which he shared with Rickman. "Proper home from home, sarge. Every modern convenience."

It was on the starboard side, just inside the forecastle. One stepped through a doorway into a brief alleyway, then through another doorway on the right, and there was the cabin. It was cramped, and it was of a peculiar shape because one side of it had to conform to the curve of the ship's bows. On that side were the two iron bunks, one above the other. There was little furniture — one wooden stool, no table, a round iron stove with a flue-pipe going up through the deckhead, and an oil lamp hung in gimbals.

"Why that?" Mason asked.

"The electricity isn't always on," Gates explained. "So then it's oil or nothing."

The cabin did not appear to have been painted recently; the bulkheads were supposed to be white, but they were in fact of a yellowy tinge with streaks of rust showing through beneath the rivets. There was one porthole to admit light and air — a task which it performed with only partial success — and one small electric bulb close to the upper bunk.

There was no order in the cabin; clothes and kit were lying all over the place. Gumboots and ammunition boots were scattered about the floor, a dirty towel was draped over the rail of the lower bunk, two oilskin coats and two souwesters hung from a nail driven into the door, a wooden packing-case that was obviously used in place of the non-existent table was littered with enamel mugs and plates, a much-thumbed copy of *Picture Post*, two Penguin novels with the covers ripped off, a half-empty tin of cigarettes and an Artillery cap-badge white with dried metal polish that had not yet been rubbed off. On top of the stove was a tin that had once contained peaches but which now held only some dirty shaving-water that somebody had forgotten to empty.

Mason drew the sole of his boot along the floor. He could hear the grit grinding under it. He supposed the floor might once have been painted, but there was now too thick a covering of dirt to allow any sign of this.

He said sardonically: "You had it all ready for inspection. Did Betts ever look in here?"

Gates looked uncomfortable. "The bombardier ate his meals in here when it was raining. There's no mess-room, you know.

"And where did he eat when it wasn't raining?"

"On the hatch. We mostly eat out there when the weather's good."

"Regular picnic parties," Mason said. "Pleasure trips and alfresco meals — just what the doctor ordered. Wonderful set-up."

"This is a coaster," Gates said, as though that statement explained everything.

"It's an old one, too. Some of the new motor-ships are all right — proper gunners' quarters, proper sanitary arrangements, and all that; but these old ones are mostly like this."

"You've done a lot of coasting?"

"A fair bit. I like deep-sea best, though. You get about more, see different places. Another thing, I'm often seasick in coastal waters — never seem to have time to get over it. One foot on sea, one on shore — neither one thing nor yet the other."

Mason looked at the littered grimy cabin with distaste. It looked as though under Betts' command it had been a case of dirty quarters as well as dirty guns. Things could certainly do with a deal of tightening up, and he would see that they had it.

"Where do you wash?"

"On deck," Gates said. "In a bucket." He was watching the expression on Mason's face, and seemed to be deriving a certain puckish delight from outlining the primitive domestic arrangements of the ship.

"Bath?" Mason said.

"Same place if you must have one."

"In full view of spectators on Tower Bridge. Isn't there any sort of wash-place?"

"There's a cubicle over on the port side that's got some kind of a shower, but I never knew anybody use it."

"Why not?"

"It's full of rope," Gates said.

"Well, at least I suppose there's a lavatory. Or is that too much to expect?"

Gates grinned, exhibiting the entire white fence of his Army teeth. "Oh, there'a lavatory all right, but you have to know the drill."

Mason was patient. "Let's have it."

"Well, it's like this — the flush don't work, so first thing you do is drop a bucket over the side on the end of a rope and get yourself a dollop of water. Then you've got something to swill down with."

"I see — and suppose the ship's moving? You get a good drag on the bucket, don't you?"

"We lose a few," Gates admitted.

★ ★ ★

44

The naval ratings came back on board shortly before midday. They were both what Mason mentally termed kids; the gunlayer, Sims, perhaps a little older than the seaman-gunner, whose name, Vickers, seemed particularly apt. Sims was taller even than Mason, possibly six foot three or four. He had a dark, thin face and an earnest expression. Conscientious type, was Mason's immediate judgment. He understood now why the twin Oerklikon was faultless.

"I've had a look at your gun," Mason said. "It's in good order. I'll stick to the same arrangement for manning — you and Vickers on the twin, myself and the other three on the bridge guns. All right?"

"Yes, sergeant." Sim's voice was quite expressionless. He did not seem to resent having to take orders from an Army N.C.O.

"You got your pay all right?"

"Yes, sergeant."

They were a little wary of him — watchful, but prepared to be friendly. Vickers was a freckled, chubby-faced, red-haired boy, the briefness of his service revealed by the dark blue of his collar, which had not yet been faded by much washing to that degree of paleness beloved by the young sailor.

Mason went along to the cabin that Sims and Vickers shared aft. He was not surprised to find that it was clean and tidy. The two bunks left very little spare room, but compared with the chart-room and fo'c'sle accommodation it was luxurious. Somebody — Mason suspected it was Sims — had knocked together a small bookcase and screwed it to the wooden bulkhead opposite the door. He glanced at the titles of the books. Between them the two sailors appeared to have catholic tastes — a paperback of *No Orchids for Miss Blandish* rubbed shoulders with a cheap edition of *The Last Chronicle of Barset.*

"Which of you reads Trollope?"

Sims said: "Oh, that's mine."

"You like it?"

"Why, yes, I do. It's like getting back to calm and sanity after all this madness. It seems to soothe the nerves — " He broke off, reddened, and looked uncomfortable, as though he felt that

46

he had made a fool of himself.

Vickers said, the statement explaining everything: "Simmy's going to be a teacher. He's got brains, haven't you, Simmy?"

"Don't be such a damned idiot," Sims told him.

Mason tapped *The Last Chronicle of Barset* with his finger. "I'd be glad to borrow this when you've finished with it. I think I could do with a bit of calm and sanity."

He knew by the way Sims's face lighted up that he had got the gunlayer on his side.

★ ★ ★

Mason ate his dinner in the open air with the sun glinting down hotly on the deck and the wharfside cranes like a forest of weird trees in the background. He used the hatch as both a table and a chair, the tarpaulin stretched over it, and clamped to the coaming with iron bars and timber wedges, making a rough, soot-grimed tablecloth — one that would have accommodated a banquet.

47

He had collected his dinner from the small galley amidships where the cook, a thin, sombre, unshaven man with a glass right eye, dispensed food with as gloomy an air as if he had been dishing out allowances of poison. The glass eye stayed disconcertingly still while the good one moved so rapidly in its watery socket that it might have been supposed to be doing double the usual amount of work in order to make up for the immobility of the other.

"He don't miss anything, though," Gates said. "You can't pull a fast one on old cookie, even if his starboard riding lamp has gone out."

The cook wore an old pair of Army denim trousers, worn-out tennis shoes, and a cotton singlet so perforated with holes that it revealed as much pale, unhealthy-looking skin as it covered. He had a lank piece of hair falling down over his forehead and a bald patch at the crown which seemed to have been worn smooth by the constant rubbing of greasy fingers. He was a slap-bang kind of man, doing everything, as it were, under protest: he banged the saucepans on the stove, slapped the bacon into the frying-pan, slapped mashed potatoes on to the seamen's plates, and kicked ineffectually at the ship's cat — all with the same air of miserable hopelessness, and with the bright glass eye shining like a sucked sweet.

Gates, who had appointed himself Mason's interpreter of the ways of coasters, explained that cooks were not as a rule present on board such ships. "This is a special arrangement for the invasion lark. Usually the crew buy their grub ashore and do their own cooking. Bit of a scramble in the galley at times — every man for himself. Personally, I'd rather have somebody do my cooking for me. I haven't got the Boy Scout mentality — not these days."

"I'd fancy somebody a bit cleaner than this bird."

"Oh, you're asking for something there. You got to take things as they are and not worry too much about the state of the cook's hands — nor what goes into the stew."

Gates eased himself off the hatch, waddled to the bulwark, and emptied the remnants from his plate into the river. From nowhere a dozen seagulls swooped upon the food, screaming and fighting.

"There's table manners for you," Gates said. "They don't care a damn whether the cook wipes his nose on his sleeve or spits in the pudding."

★ ★ ★

Early in the afternoon the *Radgate* pulled herself free from the other ships by Hay's Wharf and slipped down-river. She went without the aid of tugs, for she needed none, being able to manoeuvre almost as nimbly as a tug herself. She went down through the Pool and Limehouse Reach, past the West India Dock Pier and the Glengall Causeway and the Victoria Victualling yard, past Greenwich Pier and the Royal Naval College, Dudgeon's Wharf and Blackwall Point, the muddy river water rippling at her bows and the thin, expanding pennant of her smoke drifting away to mingle with and be lost in the great torrent that flowed from factory and engine-yard and power-station, creeping skywards to surround with a haze of dust and grit the fat balloons burning with a silver fire in the rays of the afternoon sun. She vibrated gently under the beat of her engines, their throbbing like the throbbing of a pulse beneath her skin; and now and then she gave a blast on her whistle as though she were crying out to all those who might have stood in her way that her holds were full of high explosive, and that they did so at their peril. So she came down by Greenwich Marshes and Christie's Wharf and into Woolwich Reach, where she executed a graceful turn and edged slowly towards a mooring-buoy that floated on the water like an old steel drum thrown overboard from a passing steamer.

Two men in a rowing-boat, who, one might have supposed, had been waiting there all day with this one task in view, carried the *Radgate*'s cable to the mooring-buoy and made it fast to the ring; and there she came to rest in sight of the Woolwich Free Ferry on the one hand and the warehouses of Silvertown on the other, with her stern pointing towards the sea and the

51

thin wisp still drifting from her funnel like the evidence of a schoolboy's illicit smoking.

Mason supposed there must have been some reason for the move, but he could see none. It was as though they had steamed down from Hay's Wharf to Woolwich for the sole purpose of exercising the engines, or perhaps to give the pilot a job.

Half an hour later Captain Garner sent word that he was going ashore, and would take Sergeant Mason with him to sign on at the shipping office.

3

No Hurry Back

CAPTAIN GARNER dressed for going ashore was a different man from Captain Garner in soiled overalls, ready for any task that might claim his attention on board ship. Now he might have been a commercial traveller — if one could have imagined a commercial traveller with such a dark, sunburnt face, so massive, squat and belligerent-looking, so lacking all the ingratiating ways of the man who has something to sell. But his clothes would have been correct for the job, for he wore a neat blue serge suit, a spotlessly white shirt and collar, a dark blue tie, black shoes, and a bowler hat. In his hand, as if to complete the commercial touch, he carried a small leather attache-case.

Mason was waiting for him on the foredeck when he came down the ladder from the bridge with the

Alsatian following him.

"Ready, sergeant?"

"Yes, sir."

"Right, then. Let's be moving."

A rowing-boat was waiting at the ship's side. Garner handed his attache-case down to the boatman, then climbed nimbly over the bulwark and down a short length of Jacob's ladder into the boat. Without hesitation Cerberus jumped after him, landing sure-footedly on the bottom boards.

"Still got your hanimal, I see, capting," the boatman remarked, showing tobacco-stained teeth in an ingratiating grin. "Ain't lost 'im overboard nor nuffink."

"Got more sense," Garner said, in his harsh, crow-like voice. "Him, too." he looked up at the ship's side. "Come on now, sergeant. No time to waste."

Mason came down the ladder quickly, stepped into the boat, and sat down on one of the thwarts. The Alsatian sat on its haunches in front of him, tongue lolling.

"Soldiers in ships," the boatman said, beginning to row. "There's a bloody queer idea — seems to me. What you say, capting?"

54

Garner said nothing. He was staring at the shore, ignoring the boatman, busy with his own thoughts and apparently not in any mood for small talk. The oars dipped and came up, and the water dripping from their blades was suddenly transformed by the sun into drops of molten silver.

"Like 'aving sailors in aeroplanes," said the boatman, pursuing his line of thought. He was an oldish man with an old peaked seaman's cap on his head, and he fixed Mason with a rheumy, slightly disapproving eye, as though unable to accept this incongruity of a soldier turned sailor. He shook his head. "Not right. Not right, somehow." He appeared to resent the very idea.

The shipping office was a gloomy building in which a perpetual twilight seemed to prevail — perhaps because the windows had not been cleaned, perhaps because there were not enough of them anyway. Along one side of the room into which Captain Garner led Mason was a long counter, rather like that of a bank or post-office; there was, in fact, something strangely bank-like about the whole appearance of the place; it had a banky smell of paper and ink and ledgers, a low, conspiratorial hum of conversation, the occasional chink of coins and the intermittent thump of rubber stamps. It had an air of knowing all about trade and commerce, all there was to know about ships and the men who sailed in them. It might be dingy and stuffy and badly lighted, but it knew what was what, and had a very good idea of its own importance in the scheme of all things maritime.

There were other ship's captains transacting business — some, like Garner, disguised as ordinary citizens and yet beneath all their landsmen's suiting contriving somehow to look peculiarly seamanlike — others resplendent in blue jackets with gold-braided sleeves that put Mason in mind of deep-sea ships setting out for Africa or America or Australia. He wished he were going with them, away on a long run instead of being assigned to a wretched little coaster with no cabin and nowhere to sleep but a dog-used settee in the chart-room.

The clerk filling in particulars on the

printed form glanced up at him with a grin when he gave the name of his previous ship.

"Did you say *Mauretania*?"

"Yes."

"You notice the difference?"

Mason did not answer. He was getting rather tired of that remark. What did it matter really — *Mauretania* or *Radgate*? They were both ships, both constructed with the same care, the same pride in craftsmanship. He signed his name with a pen that sent blots of ink spluttering over the form.

"There's no hurry back," Garner said. "Take the rest of the day ashore, sergeant. Enjoy yourself while you've got the chance. Won't be too much shore leave for a while, so take what you can get."

Mason headed for the West End; there was not much amusement round the Woolwich and Silvertown area. It took him over an hour to reach Piccadily, and he wondered after all whether it had been worth the effort. The West End was a cauldron of uniforms — khaki and blue and olive green — a great stew of nationalities, of Servicemen seeking relaxation. Mason had a meal in a Y.M.C.A. canteen and went to sleep in a chair. At nine o'clock he was back in Canning Town.

He decided to have a drink before rejoining the ship; it was a warm evening, and his throat was dry; he had been smoking too heavily, trying to turn his tongue into a kipper. He found himself in a street of grimy, soot-blackened houses with here and there a shop-window to break the monotony. He passed a fish-and-chip saloon and caught the warm, penetrating odour of frying; he could hear the sharp crackle as a batch of freshly chipped potatoes was doused in the boiling fat.

Two girls came out of a doorway, stared provocatively into Mason's face and went past, eating chips from a paper bag. He guessed that they were about fifteen, and trying to make themselves look older. He caught his foot in a piece of greasy newspaper that came fluttering along the pavement in a sudden gust of wind, and the paper wrapped itself round his leg and clung there until he stooped and pulled it away. He could hear the two girls giggling behind him, but when he turned they walked away.

There was a public house on the next corner, an ornate relic of the Edwardian era with peeling paint outside and a profusion of mirrors, china beer-pulls, and marble-topped tables within. Mason pushed his way into a tight pack of bodies smelling of stale sweat and a hot haze of tobacco smoke and beer fumes, edging his way to the bar with a crab-like, sideways movement. By the time he reached the beer-swilled zinc counter he was feeling hot and sticky. He waited patiently to catch the eye of one of the barmaids, then ordered a pint of bitter.

"Sorry, luv; no bitter. Not till Friday."

"Mild, then."

"Got a glass, luv?"

She was a scraggy woman with a sharply pointed chin and a long upper lip, rather like the flap on a letter-box. She looked hot, overworked, and untidy.

"I haven't got a glass," Mason said. "I've only just come in."

"You'll have to wait till somebody's finished with theirs — that's all. We're short of glasses. Can't get them, you know — not at any price."

Mason stood by the bar trying to see whether anybody looked like finishing with a glass. Nobody did. Nobody in that press of bodies semed to have any intention of leaving the place until closing-time. Whenever a man came to the bar he clung tightly to his glass until it was taken to be refilled. One of them remarked to Mason that it was bloody bad business: "People break the mugs, see. Then it's hell an' all of a job to get new ones. You may get a glass, mate; somebody may slip off 'ome. But if you was to arst me, I'd say you'd be lucky if you was to get a drink tonight. It's a bloody shame, that's what it is. The Government oughter do something." He was sympathetic, but not to the extent of offering to lend Mason his glass. He had it filled, and edged away into the press.

Mason was just about to give it up as a bad job and try another public house when a pint mug was pushed at him from the side.

"There you are, soldier. Get yourself a drink."

It was a girl's voice. Mason looked at the mug, looked at the hand holding it, looked along the bare white arm, and saw the girl. She was, he judged, about eighteen, possibly twenty; certainly no more. He had to look down at her because she was, if anything, a little below the average height for a woman, and he was tall. He did not take the mug at once; it had some beer in the bottom; he thought perhaps she meant him to drink those dregs, and he would not do that. He just stood looking down at her, his hands at his sides.

"Go on," she said. "You want a glass, don't you? Well, take it. Buy yourself a drink."

She was smiling at him, half mocking. She was not pretty. Mason was never able to say to himself with perfect honesty that she was — and Mason was a man who liked to be honest with himself. Her face was thin — too thin; her body too, as though she did not have enough food, or as though she had grown up so fast that the flesh had never had time properly to clothe her bones. She was pale also, like a flower that has seen too little of daylight and sunshine; and her brown hair was cropped short almost like a boy's. Her nose was small, but she had a wide mouth and large, wide-set eyes that looked at Mason with the perfect candour of a child. She was, he thought, all mouth and eyes, all mouth and eyes.

Her voice, not exactly harsh, had a certain metallic quality. To Mason it seemed to have echoes of voices he had heard in the country, voices of women who had much to do with horses, women in expensive tweeds with dogs at their heels. Yet this voice was not truly like those; it was not so loud, so domineering; it was, indeed, a small voice, small and rather thin like the girl herself. It was, too, a London voice, without culture. But the metal was there, brittle. It was like a voice heard over the telephone, yet without the impersonality of the telephone voice. It fitted the girl exactly.

She was still looking at him with that trace of mockery about her mouth. Her lips were slightly parted, revealing white teeth, not completely even, completely symmetrical like man-made ones, but good. Mason noticed that the lips were not painted. He noted many things about the girl in those first brief moments of seeing her, with the hum of talk going on all round them, the clink of glasses, the rattle of coins, the sudden bursts of laughter, and over all the blue-grey haze of tobacco smoke. He noticed that her eyebrows did not curve smoothly, but seemed almost angular, almost like circumflex accents that had been placed there to draw attention to the eyes. He noticed the pointedness of her chin, and a smudge of dirt in the hollow of her throat, as though some one had wiped a dirty finger there. He noticed that her cotton dress had been washed and ironed many times until the colour had faded like the colour in a tropical shirt that has been dried too often in the sun.

He lifted his hand and took the beer mug. "Thanks," he said.

She gave a laugh. "Thought you were never going to take it. You look as if you could do with a drink. You look hot."

Mason asked: "Can I get something

for you? What would you like?"

She shook her head. "Nothing. Thanks all the same. You save your money, soldier. You buy your drink. I've had all I want."

Mason had the mug filled and took a pull at the beer. It was warm and flat — hardly worth the trouble of getting. But it was wet; it eased his throat.

The girl was still at his side; she was looking at the anchor flashes on his sleeves and the crossed guns of the gunlayer's badge.

"You off a ship?"

He answered briefly: "Never mind that," and there was an inflexion in his voice that told her this was no subject to pursue.

"All right. I don't want to know anything. You don't have a cigarette, do you?"

Mason unbuttoned his pocket and pulled out a squashed cardboard packet. He watched the girl's fingers groping for the cigarette; they were thin, bony, with short-clipped nails; they looked rough, as though they were used to manual work. She found the cigarette and put it in her mouth. Mason took one for himself and lit the two with a chromium-plated lighter that he had bought in Rio de Janeiro. It was flat and neat, and it worked unfailingly. The girl admired it. She was still admiring it when a man pushed his way through the crowd, planted himself in front of her, and demanded: "Where's my mug, kid?"

Mason would have guessed that he was a docker; he seemed the type. He was not tall, but he had powerful shoulders that might have been developed by lifting heavy weights. He looked about forty, with a little grey in his hair like the scattering of hoar-frost on a lawn. He had strong features, not ugly, not handsome — just features. And he was more than half drunk, ready to pick a quarrel with anybody.

"Where is it, kid?"

"The soldier's using it."

"I told you to keep an eye on it. I told you, di'nt I?"

"Well, and so I have. I can still see it."

The man's face turned a deeper red than it had already been. "Bloody funny.

You're so smart you oughter be on the wireless." He turned on Mason. "What you mean, squaddie, takin' my mug?"

Mason did not like the man's attitude; it was belligerent. He resented the attempt to browbeat him. If the man had been less aggressive he might have answered him with more tact. As it was, he made no attempt to be placating.

"Is it yours? I thought it belonged to the house."

"That's right," another man put in. "He's got you there, Dave. One up for the sergeant."

Dave looked sour; he was clenching and unclenching his hands, as though he would have liked either to grip Mason's neck or punch him on the jaw, and could not make up his mind which to do.

"That mug had my beer in it. What you done with that? Drunk it?"

"I wouldn't dirty my mouth," Mason said. He drained the mug, set it down on the bar, and began to push his way towards the door. He was on the pavement before he realized that Dave was following him. The docker — if he was a docker — came out into the fresh

66

evening air, letting the door of the public house swing shut behind him.

"You're a damn smart boy, ain't you? A damn sight too smart. But you don't know what's good for you."

Mason saw trouble coming. He could tell when a man was spoiling for a fight, with the drink in him making him bold and quarrelsome. Mason was not one to go around looking for trouble, but when it came his way he seldom tried to dodge it. He dropped his half-smoked cigarette and ground it to shreds under the sole of his boot. If this fellow Dave wanted a fight, by God he could have it.

"What makes you so sure of that?"

He saw the girl slip out of the public house behind Dave and stand there, leaning against the wall, smoking. It was growing dusk, the outlines of the buildings losing their hardness, becoming less squalid under the softening influence of the approaching night.

"What makes me think so? I'll tell you, squaddie. Because you don't have no concern for your health, see? Because you drink my beer and pinch my mug, see? Because you try to make a fool of

67

me in front of everybody, see? That's what makes me think you don't know what's good for you."

Mason's hands were hanging easily at his sides. He was watchful. "You talk too much. You need a silencer."

He saw the girl shift her position against the wall; saw the tip of her cigarette glow red as she inhaled. He wondered what she and this fellow Dave had in common.

"Bastard squaddie," Dave said. "You think you own the bloody earth just because you got a uniform. You an' your stripes an' your badges like a perishin' Boy Scout. You're the boys — taking it nice an' safe an' easy while us civvies was doing the real work, being bombed to hell by the Jerries."

"What was the trouble? Couldn't you get away? Didn't they give you an Anderson shelter?"

He spoke with the object of stinging the man, of goading him. He was sick of talk. Get it over and to hell with it.

Dave moved quickly — more quickly than Mason had expected. What was more, he had taken his eyes off the fellow

68

for a fraction of a moment, because the girl had moved, as if she were coming forward to intervene. The movement took his eye only for the briefest interval of time, but it was enough to throw him off his guard. He jerked his head to one side, but it was too late to miss the blow altogether. Dave's fist glanced along his cheekbone, jarring the entire framework of his skull.

It made him angry. Until then he had been cool; now the anger flamed up in him. He drove his left fist hard into Dave's belly, and heard him grunt with pain as the wind was driven out of his body. Dave's head came down and Mason followed with his right. He had aimed for the jaw, but he was not completely balanced, and the fist struck Dave in the mouth. Mason felt the teeth rip his knuckles as if he had struck the steel jaws of a rabbit-trap. The shock of pain went up his arm like an electric current.

Dave was down, vomiting in the gutter, beer coming up and mingling with the blood from his gashed lip. He looked as if he had had enough already. It was the blow in the belly that had done the job; it had really hurt him. The punch in the mouth had hurt too, but that was the kind of pain that made you mad, spoiling for more fight; the other, the agony in the stomach, took the fight out of you.

Mason knew this. He knew that he was a fool to have struck at Dave's face; he ought to have kept to the body, the soft parts where the fist could sink in without harm to itself. But he had been angry, his anger had blinded him, and now he had smashed his right hand — how badly he could not yet tell.

He looked at it. It was covered with blood, some of which might be Dave's but most of which must be his own. It was running down the fingers and dripping from the tips in bright red drops. The hand was throbbing; it felt as if he had thrust it into a furnace. He tried to move the fingers and felt the pain across his knuckles. But the fingers moved all right; he did not believe that any bone was broken.

"Come away — quick — before he gets up."

The girl had come up beside him and

was tugging at his sleeve. He thought she looked scared.

"Come on. What you waiting for?"

Dave was still making retching noises, lying on the pavement and holding his stomach. Two urchins, who ought to have been in bed, had appeared from nowhere and were gazing down at him as at some interesting phenomenon. Soon there might be more people collecting, and Mason did not want to become more deeply involved. He wanted to get back to his ship.

He began to walk away, holding the damaged hand at a little distance from his body so that the blood should not drip on to his uniform. The wretched beer that he had drunk seemed to be fermenting; he could feel the gas bubbles rising, bursting in his throat, stinging the back of his nose.

When he had turned a corner and was out of sight of the public house he found that the girl was still with him. He realized suddenly that she was speaking to him, had in fact been speaking to him for some time, though he had not been listening.

"You'd better go home," he said.

He stopped walking, trying to get at his handkerchief with his left hand. The right hand was now completely covered with blood. From its appearance it might have been crushed in a machine.

The girl said: "You can't go away with your hand like that. You better come with me. I'll fix it up."

"Go back to your pal. Fix him up." Mason was feeling savage. If it had not been for this girl he would not now be nursing a smashed hand.

She answered with sudden vehemence: "He's not my pal. Him! Where'd you get that idea?"

"He called you kid. Does he go about calling anybody kid? He told you to keep an eye on his beer mug."

The girl made no direct reply; she was looking again at Mason's hand. "You better let me do something about that. Don't be a fool. You might get blood poison or something."

The idea had occurred to Mason. He had not liked the look of Dave's mouth. Supposing there should be some infection? He told himself not to start imagining things. What infection could he catch from Dave's teeth? Nevertheless, it might be as well to have the hand cleaned up as soon as possible, and he did not know how long it would take him to get back to the ship. Perhaps it would be best to go with the girl.

"How far is it?"

"Not far. I'll show you."

"All right," he said ungraciously. "But you'd better walk on my left side or you may be getting blood on your dress. You don't want that."

"No, I don't want that."

She had said it was not far, but Mason reckoned they must have walked three-quarters of a mile, perhaps more, through the jig-saw puzzle of darkening streets that made up the sprawl of this part of London. He was lost now, completely and utterly lost, following the girl blindly through this jungle of bricks and mortar, timber and concrete.

Now that the light was fading, the blackout shutters going up in the houses, he could see her at his side only as a shadowy figure — one out of the millions of Londoners, one whom, of

73

all those, chance had thrown across his path. Little more than an hour ago he had never seen her, did not know that she existed; now she was taking him to her home to wash his smashed hand. Why? he asked himself. Why did she trouble herself about him? Was it because she felt responsible for what had happened? Or was she simply kind-hearted? He did not know the answer, but he had put himself in her hands, and he followed her blindly.

"Here it is," she said.

Mason looked up at the building, at the sheer, featureless cliff of the wall and the blank eyes of the shuttered windows. There was a gap in the frontage on the left-hand side of it, a gap that had been torn out by a bomb, and now was just a waste of brick and rubble. In the gathering darkness Mason could not see very far, but he could picture in his mind what the gap looked like; there were so many gaps of the same kind that had been torn out of rows of houses — here and in other towns. There would be the sad piles of bricks and mortar, perhaps a piece of wall with some of the paper still adhering to it, the blackened outline of a chimney, a few stumps of charred timber, paths flattened out by the feet of children or people taking a short cut, and over all the merciful, creeping growth of weeds and wild flowers, blurring the marks of destruction, bringing colour to the scene of desolation.

"You better keep close behind me," the girl said. "It's dark inside."

The door was standing open and it was like going into a cave. There was a stench of dry rot, of drains, of ancient cooking, of mildewed walls: it caught at Mason's nostrils; it was heavy, sickening, making the drawing of breath an unpleasantness.

"It's upstairs — two flights. Keep close."

He followed closely at her heels. There was no carpet on the stairs, and they creaked underfoot. Mason touched a banister, but it trembled under his hand and he did not trust his weight to it. They came to a landing, turned, and mounted the second flight. Here and there a thin crack of light was visible at the foot of a door. Mason heard the muffled sound of a man talking, but the voice faded as he went on up the stairs. Somewhere he could hear a mouth-organ; it seemed a long way away, and in his mind he had a picture of the old house stretching out like an octopus in long, dark corridors, the rooms like hundreds of little cells each holding its secret, each gradually decaying, giving off the heavy odour of rottenness that filled the building.

They came to the second landing. Mason felt the girl's hand on his arm. "This way." She had lowered her voice, as though it would have been wrong to speak loudly in that dark and gloomy atmosphere. She went a little way along what Mason took to be a passage, stopped, and seemed to be groping for a door-handle. Then she pushed the door open and said: "Come on in; but don't strike a match or anything. The black-out's not up."

Mason went in and heard her shut the door behind them. He could see nothing but the vague grey outline of the window. The girl brushed past him, and he could hear her fumbling in the darkness; then he saw her head and

76

shoulders silhouetted briefly against the background of the window. A moment later the square of half-light had been blotted out by the black-out board.

He heard her voice: "Switch the light on now. It's by the door."

He groped for the switch but could not find it. The wall felt damp under his searching fingers. The girl brushed past him again. "Here: I'll do it."

The switch clicked and the room sprang into view in all its slovenliness, like a tramp suddenly revealed by the probing beam of a policeman's torch. It was not a large room, but there was space in it for one to move about even though a bed took up part of the floor. Under the window, now concealed by the lath and cardboard black-out screen, was a sink and a cold-water tap. Two chairs, a table, a chest of drawers with a mirror on top, a wardrobe and a wall cupboard, a few shelves and a gas-ring completed the furnishing. The floor was covered with linoleum, so old and worn that in many places the ragged ends of the canvas base were showing. The walls had once been papered, but the paper had been distempered, though not thoroughly enough completely to conceal the pattern, and the whole effect was one of smeariness, of a job started without enthusiasm and abandoned uncompleted.

The girl stood watching Mason as his gaze travelled round the room; her expression was again half-mocking, as it had been when she offered him the beer mug.

"Like it?"

Mason was annoyed with himself for having been caught staring. Perhaps she had guessed the kind of impact that the room had had on him, the first impression of disgust. He spoke roughly, not answering the question, but lifting his blood-covered right hand.

"Better get this washed. Then I'll leave you in peace."

She laughed. "You're in a hurry, aren't you? I'd better heat some water."

"Cold will do."

She ignored the objection, filled a tin kettle at the tap, lit the gas-ring and put the kettle on it.

"You don't need to be in such a hurry.

Why don't you sit down? The chairs won't bite you. You look silly standing there."

Mason sat on a chair that was exuding stuffing from its covering of American cloth. He could feel the springs in it.

"Where's the rest of the family?"

The girl gave him a quick glance, as if wondering whether he were serious. "Whose family? Mine?"

"Yes."

"I've got no family. None. And I don't need one." She sounded defiant. Mason let the question drop.

"What's your name, then?"

"Josephine. It's a silly name, isn't it? Most people call me Josie."

"I don't like Josie," Mason said. "I'll call you Jo."

"Please yourself. What do I call you?"

"Peter."

"All right, then. Now we've been introduced and everything's above board."

Mason grinned suddenly. "You're a funny girl, Jo."

She wrinkled her nose. "I don't know that I like that. What's so funny about me?"

79

"Let it pass," Mason said. "How about seeing to this hand?"

"The water isn't hot."

"Hot enough. You don't want to cook it."

She poured the water into a bowl, took a bottle of antiseptic from the cupboard and added a few drops to the water. Mason got up from the chair, rolled up his sleeve, tested the temperature of the water with his finger, and plunged the right hand into it. He felt the sharp sting of the antiseptic as it went into the cut, and the water turned red. Jo's head went down over the bowl as she examined the wound.

"It's not so bad as I thought. The blood made it look worse. How does it feel?"

"All right." Mason was looking at the top of her head, at the close-cropped brown hair. There seemed to be strands of gold in it; it had almost a reddish glow under the electric light. He wondered where she came from. Surely she was not entirely alone in the world, without ties of any kind? And yet, why not? She had said that she had no family. Why should she not have been telling the truth? But it was strange to come across a human unit completely detached. He wondered what her other name was. She had not told him, perhaps did not wish to tell him. Well, that was fair enough. He would not ask her. He had not told her his other name either. They were just Peter and Jo. It was enough. They were quits.

"You're a hard hitter," Jo said; and Mason thought he detected a note of admiration in her voice. "Do you often hit like that?"

"Only when it's necessary."

"It's just as well to know how to look after yourself."

"I was a fool," Mason said. "I shouldn't have hit him in the face. A fellow like that — you can hurt him more in the belly, and you don't damage your hands."

"You made a mess of him, anyway."

"Who was he?"

"I don't know. I told you I didn't. Don't you believe me? Do I have to cross my heart?"

"Why did he ask you to mind his beer?"

"Why shouldn't he? What's it got to

do with you, anyway? What difference does it make?"

"No difference. None at all. So you didn't know him?"

"No."

Well, perhaps she was telling the truth. Certainly she had shown no eagerness to stay and attend to Dave's injuries. It had been his adversary's hand that she had been worried about.

"There, it's clean enough now. I'll tie it up for you."

She dried the hand on a towel and bound it up with a piece of rag. "It's not neat, but it'll do, I think."

"It's fine," Mason said. He hesitated, not feeling so keen now to get away, to leave the girl. Maybe he would never see her again. She was a funny kid, but there was something about her . . . "I'd better go. It's getting late."

"Do you think you can find your way back to your — to wherever it is you have to go?"

"I can try." But Mason was thinking it was going to be the devil's own job to thread his way through those dark, featureless streets. He knew very little of this part of London; and even if he had known it would have been difficult finding the way in the complete darkness of the black-out. Jo noticed his hesitation.

"I think I'd better help you. I brought you here, and I expect I shall have to get you out again. You don't want to be wandering about all night."

"I can manage," Mason said.

"Of course you can. Who's saying you can't? But you'd find it easier with a guide."

Mason laughed. "You're really looking after me. Do you do this sort of thing for any soldier?"

She was angry suddenly. He could see that by the darkening of her face, the tightening of her mouth. The remark must have cut her.

"Of course; of course. Anybody. Any tramp. You didn't think you were special, did you?"

The temper had flared up in her quickly, like a match which you rubbed with the right substance to bring it into flame. Mason's words had done the rubbing, the igniting.

"I don't know why I trouble with you," she said bitterly. "You ought to be grateful instead of standing there like somebody that thinks he owns the earth."

"Do I look like that?"

"I don't know what you do look like. Anyway, it's nothing to me. Yes, you'd better go. Go and get lost if you want to. Go and walk about the streets for the rest of the night. You'll be clever if you find your way out. But what's that to me?"

She was breathing rapidly, her small, firm breasts rising and falling, reflecting the turbulence of the sea. She no longer looked so child-like. Perhaps, Mason thought, she was older than he had supposed. On a sudden impulse he put his hands under her armpits, lifted her almost off her feet, and kissed her wide mouth.

She became suddenly passive, as though all the temper were being drawn out of her by the contact of their lips. Her eyes were closed. When he released her she did not open them. She said: "You can do that again. I like it."

He kissed her again — more satisfyingly.

He closed his own eyes too, shutting out the squalor of the room.

"You don't have to go yet," she said. "You don't want to go, do you?"

"No," he said. "I don't want to go."

Captain Garner had said there was no hurry back.

4

No Shore Leave

THE tide was low when Mason went back to the ship. Mud was visible like melting chocolate — shining, slimy, glutinous. Everything he touched was damp and chilly, like the walls of a cellar.

"You're an early bird," the boatman said. "Or is it late?"

"Please yourself," Mason said.

He got into the boat and sat down on a thwart, thrusting out his feet on the bottom-boards. The oars creaked in the rowlocks and the boat moved slowly towards the *Radgate*, lying motionless at her moorings.

"Had a good time, sergeant?"

"What do you think?"

"Me? I think you're a bit of an oyster. Don't talk about yourself, do you?"

"I leave that to other people. They

usually do the job well enough — behind your back."

The boatman made a sound as though half his inside were being scraped up through his throat. He spat in the water, clearing the gunwale by an inch.

"You're right there, sergeant. They bring up the dirt when you're not there to answer for yourself. That's 'uman nature, ain't it?"

There was a mist on the river and an early-morning coolness in the air. The mist softened the outlines of the ships, making them hazy and indistinct like the objects in an impressionistic painting. The scent of the river was strong in the cool air, the scent of mud and weed and rotting timber.

"Going to be 'ot later on," the boatman said. "You mark my words — when this mist goes it'll be 'ot as blazes."

Mason fingered his chin. It was rough with stubble. He had washed but he had not been able to shave. It was bad not to be shaved; it made you feel slovenly. Shaving ought always to come first in the morning.

The boat bumped against the stained

grey side of the *Radgate*. Mason grabbed the Jacob's ladder and swung himself up to the deck. He caught a glimpse of one of the firemen going into the forecastle with an enamel dish. No one else was visible. The ship seemed not yet to have fully awakened from its night's sleep; the iron of bulwark and deck and winch was moist with condensation, the cover of the forward hatch wet and taut.

Mason went into the gunners' cabin and found Gates and Rickman eating a breakfast of fried sausage and scrambled egg. They looked up when he came in, and Gates stopped a forkful of sausage half-way to his Army issue teeth.

"Morning, sarge. You've been a long time signing on. Did you get lost?"

"Skip it," Mason said. "Is there any of that grub left in the galley?"

"Should be. You want to be quick, though." He took another look at Mason, and saw the bandaged hand and the bruise on the cheek where Dave's fist had left its mark. "Hullo, hullo! You been in a rough-house or something?"

"Something," Mason said. The smell of fried sausage was making him feel hungry. Jo had found a tin of beans and had cooked them for supper, but that had been a long while ago. Mason had a healthy appetite, and he did not believe in missing a meal if it could be helped.

Rickman was stolidly putting away sausage and egg, and washing the mixture down with tea from a pint mug. With scarcely a pause in the process he said: "You better get a move on, sarge. The cook don't keep breakfast hanging about all that long."

Mason went up to the chart-room to fetch his plate and mug, and found Cerberus asleep on the settee. The Alsatian opened one eye when Mason came in, but made no other movement. Mason wondered whether the dog had spent the night there; if so it was as well that he had slept ashore. He felt that Cerberus and he would have to come to some understanding about the sharing of the settee, for the dog obviously considerd it had a perfect right there.

He took his breakfast to the gunners' cabin. The chart-room was no place in which to eat one's meals, especially with a large dog taking up the greater part of the only seat. Gates and Rickman had finished their breakfast and were enjoying a cigarette, filling the cramped space with smoke.

"You got it all right, then," Gates said.

"The cook was a bit snotty. Didn't take kindly to my being late."

"He's like that. Don't take no notice. He's like all cooks — thinks he's the most important blighter in the ship."

"Maybe he is."

"An army," Rickman said, dragging up the memory of something one learned at school, "marches on its stomach. That's what Napoleon said."

"Bloody uncomfortable," Gates said. "You don't catch me doing any marching on my stomach. It's the wrong shape." He winked at Mason, and cleared a space on the packing-case for Mason's plate. "Put it down here, sarge. Savoy hotel ain't in it."

Rickman looked pained. "It's a figure of speech — that's what it is."

"What is?"

"Marching on your stomach. It don't

mean you slide along like a snake. It means you have to have plenty of grub inside you, else you can't fight."

Gates opened his eyes wide in mock wonder. "Is that so? And yet some people say you shouldn't take violent exercise on a full stomach."

"Well, that's different. It ain't the same thing at all."

Gates shook his head. "I don't know where you get all this book-learning from; straight I don't. You been studying in secret, Ricky? Figures of speech, Napoleon. What else?"

The sausages on Mason's plate looked as though they were suffering from disgusting skin disease; they were grey, blotchy. Mason ignored the appearance, ignored the taste, pushing this unpromising material down his throat to fill the empty spaces of his stomach.

"Where's Scarr?" he asked. "Still in his bunk?"

"He went ashore last night," Gates said. "He hasn't come on board again yet."

"Went ashore, did he? And who gave him permission?"

Gates looked uncomfortable. "Why, I don't know about that. Maybe, seeing as you weren't here, he thought it'd be all right. I believe he lives somewhere out Dagenham way. Got a wife there. Likes to get home when he can. You know how it is."

Mason said nothing. He knew how it was. He would have to have a word with Scarr when the gunner came on board.

"I hear they've started making sausages out of horsemeat," Rickman said. "We better win this war soon, else we'll all be poisoned."

"Cats," Gates said. "They been rounding 'em up for months. Got a special cat-catching service. You don't see many strays about now."

"What's going to happen about rats if they take all the cats?"

"Same thing, boy — into the old sausage-skins. You never know what you're eating when it's minced up small. For all you know, you may be a cannibal. There's a thought for you."

Mason, chewing hard, came on a piece of cloth-like substance. He pulled it out of his mouth and parked it on the side of his plate. Gates looked at it gravely. "See what I mean?" he said.

As soon as he had finished his breakfast Mason fetched some hot water from the galley and went up to the chart-room to shave. Cerberus had disappeared, leaving only some hairs and a depression in the settee as a record of his presence. Mason put the mess-tin of water on the chart-table, took a small fragment of mirror from his haversack and wedged it in a corner of the window, and proceeded to lather his face. The bruise on his cheekbone was like a smudge of paint; there was a bit of a swelling under the eye, but nothing to worry about. Nevertheless, he felt that he ought to have been able to handle a blundering swinger like Dave with more ease. He ought not to have allowed himself to be marked — not by a drunk. But perhaps Dave had not really been so drunk. Jo had said he was not.

Mason's thoughts swung back to the girl; he could not keep them away from her for long. He was being a fool no doubt; but that was the way it was. Tonight he was going to her again; he had promised, and he had no desire to break that promise. He remembered the way she had looked up at him with her wide, child-like eyes, her short hair ruffled, not combed or brushes but tousled like an urchin's, and her small nose wrinkling.

"You will come? You're sure?" He could see that she had doubts about him, that she only half expected to see him again.

"Nothing's going to keep me away."

"I'm glad," she said.

Mason nicked his chin with the razor and swore. Through the chart-room window he could see across the quarter-deck to the ship's grimy funnel and, just visible behind it, the twin Oerlikon. He decided to spend part of the morning in putting the gunners through their paces, to find out just how smart they were. You needed to know what your men could or could not do. The drill might need smartening up. He did not suppose Bombardier Betts had done much in that way.

He wondered when Scarr would turn up. He was angry with Scarr; if the fellow wanted to sneak ashore like that he should at least have made certain that he was back early in the morning. He would have to give Scarr a chewing.

The drill went better than Mason had expected. Rickman was a bit slow and not too certain of the stoppages, but Gates, surprisingly enough, was the smartest of the bunch; he seemed to know the gun inside out, knew the order of loading the magazines — tracer, non-tracer, incendiary — knew the coloured markings of British and American ammunition without reference to the book, and was able to lift a full magazine and fit it gently into place on the gun without any of the strain and struggle that Rickman and Vickers required. What any of them would be like in action Mason could not tell; you could never tell what a man would be like in action until action came; some of the most unlikely-looking material often turned out to be the best — and the other way round. He felt pretty sure, however, that he could rely on Gates.

Scarr turned up at about half-past eleven. Mason, with no other place available, was forced to give him his dressing-down in the chart-room. Scarr was sullen, justifying himself in a whining voice.

"How was I to ask your permission sarge, when you wasn't on board?"

"If you hadn't got permission you shouldn't have gone."

"But have a heart, sarge. The missus is expecting."

The statement might be true, Mason thought, and again it might not. He had a shrewd suspicion that what Mrs Scarr was really expecting was not an addition to the family but her husband's evening arrival.

"How close is it?"

Scarr mumbled something about its being close enough.

"Then why don't you apply for compassionate leave?"

"What, now, sarge? Just when the balloon's about to go up? No, I wouldn't want to do that. It wouldn't seem like playing the game somehow. Just so long as I can slip off home now and again."

Mason had had experience of a great number of gunners during his Army career, and he had never seen a man whom he would have suspected of having less concern about playing the game than Scarr. But he let it pass.

He said: "I'm going to give you a try-out on the gun — and God help you if you aren't up to the mark."

Rather to his surprise, he found that Scarr had a very good knowledge of the gun and the drill. Mason could not fault him there.

"Ever been in action — real action?"

Scarr gave his lopsided grin. "Don't know what you call real. Colliers running coal to the Channel ports — down from the Tyne through E-boat Alley. Real enough for me, I can tell you."

In the afternoon an officer, very full of his own importance, came on board to brief the guns' crews. He had a round, cherry-red face and a blond moustache which he was for ever smoothing down with his forefinger, as though trying to convince himself that it was really still there, and had not been blown away by the wind. Before leaving he said: "You know, of course, that there is no shore leave. All personnel are confined to their ships until further notice. Security and all that."

"I did not know, sir," Mason said. He thought of Jo. She was expecting him that evening, and now this damned moustache-smoother had said that no one was allowed ashore. It was the devil.

"Well, you know now," the officer said. "Any questions? No? Then I'll be pushing along. Good luck. Wish I was coming with you. It should be quite a show — yes, quite a show."

Mason watched him climb down into the launch that had brought him, watched the launch chug away. He saluted smartly and received a languid acknowledgement. "Damned fool!" he muttered. "Quite a show! What's he think it is — a kid's game? Damned little jumped-up fool with his pretty moustache and his 'Quite a show'! Wishes he was coming with us. I'll bet!"

Mason saw clearly what his resentment against the young officer sprang from — from the order about not going ashore. Where was the sense in it? Were they afraid of gunners running away? Or were they scared that vital information might leak out? As if it could. Every one knew that an invasion had been planned; they would have had to be blind and deaf not to have known. What they did not know was when and where; and as to that, the gunners and ships' crews were no wiser. This order was another piece of unnecessary petty legislation, a further infringement of liberty. Surely at this time a man ought to have been allowed all the freedom possible, since there was no telling when he would have any more. For some this might be the last chance.

He was going up to the chart-room when Captain Garner called him into his cabin. "Tomorrow," Garner said, "we're going down to Southend. This is confidential, mind. I thought I'd tell you so you could make the most of a last night ashore."

"Thank you very much, sir; but unfortunately we're confined to the ship."

"By whose orders?"

"Army orders. The officer who came on board just now told me."

Garner winked with such a laborious

effort that half his left cheek seemed to be pushing its way into his eye. "We don't have to know about things like that, do we? As long as you're back in good time in the morning I'm not worrying. But remember we leave at ten."

"I'll remember it, sir. And thank you."

It was a measure of the hold that Jo had taken on him in so brief a time that Mason should even have considered taking advantage of Garner's permission. Mason was a believer in discipline; he believed that an army could function efficiently only by a strict obedience to orders — even senseless ones. Therefore, in the ordinary way he would have stayed on board ship despite the captain's offer, and he would have seen to it that the gunners stayed on board also. As it was, when Scarr came to see him with a request to be allowed to go ashore and see his expectant wife Mason was in a quandary.

"You heard what the lieutenant said about shore leave being stopped, didn't you?"

"I heard what he said, sarge; but I don't suppose he expected us to stick to the letter of the law, as you might say. Not under the circumstances."

"What circumstances?"

"About my missus. You know."

"I only know what you told me."

"Well, you don't think I'd tell you a lie, do you, sarge? Not me. Not. R. S. Scarr."

"Since you ask me, that's just what I do think."

Scarr grinned, as if he and Mason were sharing a good joke — the joke of suspecting him of not telling the truth. "Now, now; you don't really mean that. Not really. I'm not saying as how I mightn't stretch things a bit on occasion. Who wouldn't? But not in a case like this — a case of life and death like."

Mason saw quite clearly that he would either have to let Scarr go or stay on board also. He could not refuse permission for the gunner to go ashore and then slip away himself. It would be neither just nor wise.

"If I let you go I want your word that you'll be back on board by eight o'clock in the morning." He did not tell Scarr that the ship was sailing at ten; that was a fact he had been told in confidence.

Scarr's sharp, rat-like face registered his satisfaction. "No need to worry about me, sarge. I'll be back on the dot. When I'm treated right I act right."

Mason did not reflect any of Scarr's pleasure. He knew that he had gone up in Scarr's estimation, but by an equal amount he had fallen in his own. It was for his own satisfaction alone that he had given the gunner permission to go ashore — and he had no right to give that permission; it was contrary to orders.

He said harshly, angry with Scarr and with himself: "If you aren't back on time I'll wring your blasted neck. Get out of my sight."

Scarr went before Mason could change his mind.

Later in the afternoon a batch of mail came on board. There were three letters for Mason, and he knew by the handwriting from whom each one of them came. There was one from his father, one from Phil Brightwell, a boyhood friend now serving in Burma, and the third from Clare. Seeing the small, neat, backward-sloping characters of Clare's writing, he felt a twinge of conscience. He took the letters up to the chart-room and put them on the table, but he did not open them at once. Instead he took out a cigarette and lit it, his actions deliberate, restrained. He saw this as a change in himself, and the change was due to Jo. Ordinarily he would have slit Clare's letter open at once, would have read it through eagerly. Now he left it until the last of the three.

He read his father's letter first — brief and stiff as usual; more like a report on the state of the crops and livestock than anything else. Phil's letter was longer, put together in snatches, stained with sweat, giving no news, just talking to him as Phil would have done if he had been present in person. Mason decided that it was time he wrote to Phil again; out there in Burma he must be hungry for the sense of contact with home that only letters could give. Yes, he would certainly write to Phil.

He opened Clare's letter almost hesitantly, as though he were half fearful of reading what might be in it.

Yet he knew that there was no cause for misgiving; Clare did not write the kind of love-letter that might stir up feelings of guilt. The 'Dearest Peter' with which it began and the 'All my love' which ended it were the nearest approaches to anything passionate in the whole length of four closely written sheets. The letter was full of small items of news from the village, from the two farms, Mason's and Hordern's, that adjoined each other and might some day be united into one. That certainly had been the expectation for years; every one had taken it for granted that Peter Mason and Clare Hordern would marry; it was an obvious match. Peter and Clare themselves, without ever making any formal engagement, had accepted the situation. It had seemed an obvious match to them also.

Mason could imagine Clare writing the letter, tired perhaps after a long day on the farm where she now did as much hard work as any labourer; he could picture her gold hair swept back from her forehead, the fair skin browned by the sun, the dusting of freckles on the cheeks. He could imagine the slight pucker in her forehead, the frown of concentration as she tried to remember all those small, unimportant bits and pieces of gossip that were yet so important in painting a picture of home.

'We played a game of tennis last week. The court was terribly neglected and the balls were soft as putty, but Harry Loader was home on leave, and he and Betty wanted a game. Mr Wilson made up the four — we had to rope him in, poor man. Not very high-class play — as you can imagine . . . '

Tennis! Mason tried to remember when he had last had a game. It must be years. Once he had thought of tennis and cricket as two of the most important things in life; now they had faded into the background; they were nothing, frivolous pastimes not to be reckoned beside the realities of war. He remembered how well he and Clare had played together, winning tournaments, going round in that old Morgan three-wheeler of his. And all the time Europe had been grinding towards the savagery, the agony, the madness of war.

Clare and he had grown up almost

as brother and sister. As a child she could do most things as well as any boy — things like fishing, paddling a canoe on the river that ran by the two farms, pitching a tent, lighting a camp-fire. There had never been any need to make allowances for Clare because she was a girl. It was when she was sixteen that he realized almost with a sense of shock just how attractive she was, with her thick, golden hair and the fine-cut oval of her face. It gave him a sense of pride to go into town with her and note the admiring glances that she drew. To her the fact of her beauty seemed to be quite without significance; she was completely un-self-conscious, completely without affectation.

She was seventeen when her mother died. That made one more thing that Clare and he had in common, for Mrs Mason had died two years earlier. The death of her mother had its effect on Clare's life. If Mrs Hordern had lived she would have remained mistress of the farmhouse, and Clare might have tried to make some other career for herself. As it was, she took up the reins that her mother had laid down, and ran the household so capably that her father scarcely felt the change. He was a man who spent little time indoors, always preferring to be out in the fields or in the barns or cow-shed, keeping an eye on things. He hated paper-work; forms of any sort were anathema to him. Together with the housekeeping, Clare took on the clerical side of the farm work, filling in returns, making out the wages list, dealing with correspondence. "I've given you a good education," Mr Hordern said, "a darn sight more expensive one than I ever had. Now you can make some use of it."

Hordern was a hard-working man himself, and he expected other people on the farm to work hard also. Clare did not disappoint him. Once in an expansive mood he confided in Mason: "She's worth her weight in gold to me. But don't you go telling her what I said; she'll be asking for a bigger allowance." He tapped Mason on the chest with the smooth handle of his stick. "She'll make some young farmer a good wife one of these days. A farmer, mind. I wouldn't want her to throw herself away on some damned bank clerk or shopkeeper or suchlike." He winked, rubbed his nose with the stick, and went away to look at some pigs; there was no mistaking his meaning.

Similar ideas semed to be working in the mind of Mason's father also. Albert Mason was a tall, lean man with a dark, weather-beaten face and shrewd, calculating eyes. "It'd be a fine thing for the two farms to come together," he said. "Near a thousand acres between 'em, and some of the finest land in the county. You'd have something under your hand then, son. But that won't be yet awhile," he added hastily. "I'm good for a few more years, and I don't doubt Hordern is too. Still it's something to think about."

Mason did think about it. He supposed Clare thought about it too, though neither of them said much to the other on that particular subject. Once, however, when they were returning in his car from a tennis match Clare put a hand on his arm as they reached the summit of the last hill before dipping down into the valley where the farms lay.

"Stop here a moment, please," she said.

Below them the mist was creeping up from the hollows, but the farms were still visible in the evening light — the two big houses, the outbuildings, all dwarfed by distance, the black lines of hedges, clumps of trees, the river sliding along the northern edge, the chequerboard effect of fields and meadows.

"It's beautiful," Clare said. "Don't you see how beautiful it is?"

It had never occurred to him to think of the farms as beautiful. Farming was a way of life, a method of making a living, a good method; but he had never thought of the beauty of the land. Seeing it now, as if through her eyes, he saw that it was beautiful.

"Yes," he said. "I do."

"Farming is the best life in the world," Clare said. "I don't think I should want to live away from a farm."

"Nor I."

Mist and darkness had blotted out the valley when they drove on, but he could still see the vague outline of Clare's face as she turned to smile at him, and the shadow of her hair. He could still feel the warmth of her lips and the pressure of her body against his own.

"Life is going to be fine," Clare said. "Just fine."

In Nuremberg Hitler was making one of his week-end speeches, and thousands of arms were rising in the Nazi salute. "Führer! Führer! Führer! Heil! Heil! Heil! — Heil Hitler!"

"Life is going to be fine."

Mason read Hitler's speech in the morning paper. He had already looked at the cricket scores.

"Lebensraum — the Polish Corridor — Danzig — Sudentenland — Communist hyenas — Jewish traitors — Aryan blood — the glory of the Third Reich — justice for the Fatherland — "

"Life is going to be fine."

Mason sat back, drawing at his cigarette, remembering. He remembered his last leave. He had come home unexpectedly, and there had been no time to let anyone know. He went over to Hordern's at once, walking by way of the fields, pushing through a gap in the

110

hedge between the two farms that had been there as long as he could remember. He came up to the house from the back, going through the stockyard and past the barn and cowsheds.

The back door of the house was open, and he went in without knocking and found Clare rolling out pastry on the kitchen table, a dusting of flour on the end of her nose, and a wisp of hair falling over her forehead. He rememberd the way she looked at him, hardly believing at first that he was really there, and then the delight in her face, no attempt at disguising it. He kissed her then, not caring about the flour on her nose and on her hands — soon on his uniform too.

"Clare," he said, "you're the only girl for me."

She answered breathlessly: "I hope I am, Peter. Oh, I hope I am."

"No doubt about it. Do you love me?"

"Every nice girl loves a sailor. I thought you knew that."

"I'm not a sailor."

"You're half one. That's good enough for me."

"Good enough for me too."

"How long have you got? When do you have to go back?"

"I've got fourteen days, and I'm going to spend it all with you."

"I have work to do."

"I'll help you."

He kissed her again; then held her at arm's length, gazing at her.

"You're prettier than ever. No, not pretty — beautiful. You could be a film star."

"I'm no actress, Peter."

Mason folded the letter and put it away in his pocket. He would not answer it now. Perhaps he would not answer it until after the invasion. There was nothing to say. And yet he knew that if it had not been for Jo he would have sat down and written an answer at once.

Captain Garner was playing his violin when Mason left the ship. It sounded like a lament. The door of the captain's cabin was open, and the thin notes went floating out over the river. A trim motor-vessel with a high poop was chuffing her way up-stream with the red, white, and blue striped flag of the Netherlands fluttering at her jack-staff. Four of the *Radgate*'s crew were playing cards on the forward hatch-cover, oblivious of the high-explosive ammunition stowed away below them.

Gates was watching the game. Mason drew him on one side. "I'll be back early in the morning. Has Scarr gone?"

"Half an hour ago. Have a good time, sarge. But don't go getting into any more rough-houses."

Mason's face clouded for a moment; then he grinned. Gates was all right. No need to take offence at a simple remark like that. Certainly he had no intention of getting into a fight — not with his right hand still bandaged and stiff from the cut. But he felt ashamed to be disobeying orders under Gates's knowing eye. Probably the gunner thought nothing of it, and there were plenty of N.C.O.'s who would have thought nothing of it either. Mason knew that, but it did not lessen the feeling of shame.

He gave a flip of his hand and climbed over the side to the waiting boat, following the mate and the chief engineer, two men so stout, so nearly

113

equal in height, and so peculiarly alike in appearance that one might have supposed them to be brothers. That this was not so Mason already knew. He knew also that the mate Gregory and the chief engineer Mawby were continually at loggerheads. Perhaps their dislike of each other sprang from their physical resemblance, for it must have been particularly galling for each to see in the other all those almost clownish features that he himself possessed. It was like peering into a revealing mirror, seeing the bleary eyes, the puffy cheeks, the bottle nose, the protruding bottom, and the waddling gait all too clearly portrayed.

Even their voices were strangely similar, being low-pitched, rumbling, like the sound of distant thunder. They were gloomy men, hating each other for showing what they were themselves, hating themselves for being like the picture they saw. To the crew they were known irreverently as Tweedledum and Tweedledee, and the knowledge of this fact did nothing to sweeten their already sour outlook on life.

In the boat they sat as far apart as

it was possible to be, avoiding each other's eyes.

"Been a nice day," the boatman remarked. "Sort of weather you want when you go across to the other side. Wonder what they're waiting for. If it was me to decide, I'd start right now, take advantage of the fine weather and have all the summer ahead of me. That's what I'd do."

The mate said cuttingly: "You don't happen to be in charge of operations."

The boatman was undeterred by sarcasm. "No. And there's another thing — having this Yankee general, Eisenhower, in command; that don't seem right to my way of thinking. What's wrong with Monty? That's what I'd like to know. If I was going across there I'd feel a hell of a lot safer under Monty than under any damned Yankee."

"Well, you're not going," the mate said. "So why in hell are you worrying?"

The boatman looked peeved, seemed about to retort, thought better of it, spat in the water, and shipped his oars. The mate and the chief engineer stepped out of the boat and went off in opposite directions without a word to each other, hurrying away on their stumpy legs as if the one desire of each was to put as much space as possible between himself and the other.

"There's a pair for you," the boatman said.

Mason lost his way twice in the labyrinthine streets that led him by devious and intricate ways to the tenement house where Jo had her room. By daylight it looked even more squalid than it had in the dusk of the previous evening; the bricks had a kind of yellowy, bilious appearance, as though they had at some long-ago period had been freshly painted but had gradually lost that surface gloss under the influence of time and weather. To the height of about four or five feet the walls bore witness to the activities of children — scratched initials, hollowed-out mortar, crude caricatures in chalk, and here and there the representation of cricket stumps.

The bombed site next to the house was as Mason had pictured it, but it had in the centre a piece of old sacking supported by sticks to form a rough tent, and round this a gang of children were playing Cowboys and Indians, filling the air with the shrill sound of their war-whoops.

Mason went up the stairs slowly. He could feel the excitement leaping in him despite the hold that he was trying to keep upon himself. What would it be like — this second encounter? The girl was not pretty. So what was it that had drawn him to her? Was there perhaps nothing after all? When he saw her again would the whole romantic structure fall in pieces about his feet?

A man came out of a room on the first floor, a middle-aged man with a weary, nervous look. He was dressed in patched grey flannel trousers and a blue serge waistcoat; his shirt was collarless, and when he passed Mason on the stairs he kept his eyes carefully averted, as though he felt that at some time or other he might be called upon to identify Mason, and he did not want any trouble of that sort. His feet fell softly on the bare wooden stairs, making a padded, scuffling noise as if they were wrapped round with layers of felt. Mason, looking down when he had passed, saw the top of his head where the hair was thinning, and the oil with which he had smoothed it down shining damply.

Mason reached the second floor and moved along the corridor, searching for Jo's room. Even in the daytime the light was poor, and the closed doors seemed to conceal their own peculiar secrets. To the usual heavy odour of the house was now added that of toasting cheese, as though somewhere some one were preparing a meal.

He found Jo's door and knocked lightly with his knuckles. Nobody opened it, and he could hear no sound from inside. He gave another knock, then turned the knob and pushed the door open. The room was empty. He went in and shut the door behind him.

He noticed at once that some attempt had been made at tidying the room; there were no articles of clothing lying about, and the bed had been made. He moved across to the window and looked out, but all he could see was a kind of tarred courtyard below, and on the other side of this another shabby brick building sadly in need of paint and repair.

Mason sat down in one of the chairs, lit a cigarette, and prepared to wait. He wondered how long it would be before Jo put in an appearance. Would she come straight back from work? He had promised to be there, but had she believed him? He wonderd where she worked. She had mentioned something about a factory, but only vaguely; and he had not pressed for details. He did not wish to know a lot about her; he did not wish her to know anything about himself. It would be so much better if it were left like that.

He finished one cigarette and lit another. He heard somebody go past the door, running lightly; then some one else, shuffling slowly; he heard a sudden gust of laughter, heard a door slam, then silence. Something bumped heavily on the floor above, as if some one had fallen out of bed. There was a sound as of a rat gnawing in the wall.

Mason finished the second cigarette, went to the sink, and dropped the butt down the waste-pipe. He went back to the chair and closed his eyes; the room was warm, and he felt drowsy. In a moment he had dropped off to sleep with all the ease of the soldier.

It was the opening of the door that awakened him. He sat up, wide awake at once, and saw Jo come into the room. She was breathing quickly, as though she had run up the stairs. Mason saw her face light up with happiness when she saw him. He got up from the chair and she came to him, lifting up her mouth to be kissed.

When he let her go she said: "So you came."

"Didn't you think I would? I promised."

"I know. But I was afraid you wouldn't."

"Afraid? Would it have meant so much to you?"

"I wanted you to come. Do I have to tell you that?"

"I like to hear it."

He kissed her again. Then he held her away from him, looking at her face, the soft mouth, the wide-set eyes, velvety brown, the small, flared nose and the pale skin.

"I was wrong," he said. "You are pretty."

"Wrong?"

"I thought you weren't. I couldn't have been looking."

She shook her head, pulling herself away from his hands and going to the mirror on the chest of drawer. "This face? Pretty? You don't have to tell me that nonsense. I gave up hoping I'd ever be pretty years ago."

"You are pretty."

She turned away from the mirror, laughing at him, happy. "You say it nicely, anyway. Perhaps if you say it often enough I'll end up believing it. You might even believe it yourself. That would be something, wouldn't it?"

"I don't have to convince myself. It's true."

"It must be the mirror that's at fault, then. I'll have to buy a new one. Or perhaps you will. Bring me one back from China with a silver frame and jewels. Will you?"

"If that's what you want."

"Oh, you'll promise anything. Promises are cheap. But I don't want a silver mirror — nor jewels either."

"What do you want, Jo?"

"What do I want? Oh, something that you'll never give me, my soldier boy — not ever."

"I'll give you anything — anything I can."

"Oh, no, not you. You say that, but you know it isn't true. So let's forget it, shall we? Let's talk about something else."

She went to the sink and began to wash her hands under the tap. Her legs were bare — straight and slim, like a boy's. She walked like a colt, not studying the grace of her movements, and achieving a kind of natural grace without effort.

"You been here long?" she asked.

Mason looked at his wrist-watch. "About an hour — maybe a little more."

"As long as that? I'm sorry I was late."

"I'd have waited longer than that."

"You would? For me?" She was drying her hands on a towel, laughing at him again. "Even if I'm not pretty."

"I told you you were. Have you forgotten?"

"I like to be reminded." She came with the towel in her hand, lifting her mouth up so that he should kiss her again, laughing, happy as a child at play.

"Why don't you lock your door?" Mason asked.

"The lock's broken. It should have been mended weeks ago, but it never gets done."

"Anybody could get in and steal your things."

She glanced round the room, the corners of her mouth twisting. "Who would want to pinch my things?"

"But aren't you afraid?"

"Afraid! Why should I be afraid? I can take care of myself. I've had to long enough."

She hung the towel on a cord and came back to him. "Give me a cigarette, Peter. I haven't had a smoke since morning."

He gave her one and took another for himself, lighting them both with the chromium-plated lighter that she had admired when they first met — could it be less than twenty-four hours ago? He felt as though he had known her always. She was walking about the room, restless, puffing at the cigarette, not inhaling deeply as he did, dragging the smoke down into his lungs.

"We'll get some fish-and-chips for supper," she said. "Bring them up here to eat. Do you want to go out for a drink?"

He thought of the crowded pubs, of people like Dave, people who might know Jo. He did not want that; he wanted her completely to himself; he wanted to make himself believe that there was no one else in the world that she knew except himself.

"No," he said. "I don't want a drink unless you do."

"Nor me. It's a waste, isnt it? I'll make some coffee. I'm good at coffee. You'd be surprised."

"I wouldn't be surprised at anything."

He could hear the rat gnawing in the wall again, a man whistling, a girl's voice shouting something unintelligible, footsteps, the muffled sound of music from some wireless-set. All around them people were living their lives, going about their affairs, and here in this little cell he and Jo were alone, unconcerned with all those others, living only for themselves.

"I'm glad you came," she said. "I'd have been wretched if you hadn't come. I didn't really think you would, but I'm glad you did."

"I'm glad too." What did disobedience to orders matter? It was a fool order anyway. What did it matter if he lowered himself in Gates's estimation or raised himself in Scarr's? All that mattered was being with Jo. Nothing else was worth two pins.

He said: "After tonight I shan't be able to come again for a while."

She caught in her breath suddenly, and he could see the disappointment in her face, drawing down the mobile corners of her mouth. "You're going away? How long?"

"I don't know how long. Not exactly. It may be a week, two weeks; perhaps more."

"Perhaps you'll go away for good. Perhaps I shall never see you again. Is that what you're trying to say?"

"If I don't come back you'll know I'm dead." It was a damned silly melodramatic thing to say, but perhaps it was true all the same.

"No, no; I shan't know that. I shall never know anything. I don't want to know. You just have to take what comes; take the moment. It's no good looking ahead — nor back neither. It's the now, now, now — that's all that matters."

★ ★ ★

The room was in darkness, but Mason was still awake when the door opened and closed again quietly. He could hear Jo's gentle breathing; but now there was other, heavier breathing, like that of a man panting after a race.

Mason slipped out of bed, fumbled for his trousers in the darkness, and slipped them on. Moving towards the electric-light switch, he brushed against something that yielded. A man cried out suddenly, fearfully, and then was silent. Mason switched the light on and saw, cringing against the wall, the man who had passed him on the stairs the previous evening. The man stared at Mason, his lips quivering. From outside there came the sound of heavy footsteps, of men's voices.

126

The man said, pleading: "Let me stay here. Don't let them find me."

He was shivering, as if he felt the cold. He kept looking from Mason towards the door and back again at Mason. His eyes were filled with terror. There was a trapped, hopeless look about him like that of a cornered animal.

"Who are you looking for?" Mason asked. He was angry with the man for breaking into the room, for bringing troubles with him, loading them on to other people. "Who is it?" he asked again, staring at the man's oily, ruffled hair, his lined face, his watery, frightened eyes.

The man gave a little flutter with his hands, a gesture of helplessness. The footsteps came along the corridor, halted. Someone rapped on the door, and the man's gaze went round the room as if he were searching for some place in which to hide.

"Who's that?" Mason called.

"Military police."

"What do you want?"

"We're looking for a deserter. We believe he came into this room."

The man who was speaking must have had his hand on the door-knob, for the door swung suddenly open and Mason saw that there were two of them, a sergeant and a lance-corporal, their blancoed belts and gaiters showing up whitely in the light of the room.

The man with the oiled hair gave a cry and tried to dart past them, but they were old hands at that game; they had him. If Mason had not been so angry with the man he might have been sorry for him. He was not young; he was not tough; no doubt he had been conscripted into the Army, and it had been more than he could bear. For a time he had had a nervous, hunted freedom, and now it was at an end. He would be taken back and punished — for wanting to be free. It was madness.

The sergeant was looking at Mason's trousers. "You on a pass?"

"Yes," Mason said.

"I'd better see it — and your A.B. 64."

Mason picked up his battle-blouse from the chair where he had dumped it and pulled his pay-book and the ship's pass signed by Captain Garner out of the pocket. The military policeman had noticed the stripes on the sleeves of the blouse, and his manner was slightly less stiff when he took the pass and pay-book.

"Thanks, sergeant."

He examined both of them carefully, and seemed to be puzzled by the ship's pass, as though unable to make up his mind as to whether this were valid or not. But after he had read through it twice, looked Mason up and down with a hard, military-policeman kind of stare, and glanced almost furtively at the bed, he said: "All right, sergeant. Sorry we had to trouble you. All part of the job, you know."

"I know," Mason said.

He took back his documents and waited for the room to clear. The sergeant shot one more glance at the silent Jo, turned, and said harshly: "Right, corporal. Get weaving."

With the deserter sandwiched between them they went out of the room, banging the door behind them. Mason listened to their footsteps moving along the corridor and down the stairs until they faded.

He heard a motor-engine start to life and move away into the night. Then he switched the light out.

Jo, who had not previously spoken a word, said: "They've gone."

"Yes," Mason said. "They've gone." But the question that was nagging him was why the deserter had come into the room in the first place. Why had he chosen that of all others? Had he been familiar with the room?

"Did you know him?"

"Who?"

"That fellow they arrested."

"I've seen him before."

"Why should he come in here?"

"How do I know? Perhaps it was the only room he could get into."

"You ought to have that lock seen to," Mason said.

5

Twenty-four Hours

IT was getting on for ten o'clock, the pilot was on board, and Scarr had not yet put in an appearance. Mason fumed. This finished Scarr for him; from now on he would be tough. What made him the more angry was the realization that if it had not been for his own desire to go ashore he would not have allowed Scarr to do so. Now if Scarr failed to turn up he would have only himself to blame.

Gates and Rickman, and the two naval gunners, Sims and Vickers, were all busy cleaning guns — those weapons having the peculiar property of acquiring dirt even when not in use, and protected by a waterproof cover. "Specially invented to make work," Gates said.

Mason had been along to the poop to examine some new smoke-generators that had been delivered the previous day.

They were not the big smoke-floats that merchants ships had been equipped with for years, but were like small, cylindrical oil-drums, and were for use on board the ship. Mason had had his orders concerning them: 'Only to be used if the ship is directed to make smoke.' Well, that was clear enough. He made sure that they were all securely fixed in position, read again the instructions for use, and went back to the foredeck, watching for Scarr, and cursing the gunner in his absence.

On his way he encountered Captain Garner. Garner was neither in his dungarees nor in his shore-going clothes; he had in fact dressed himself up in a brass-buttoned jacket with the gold braid of his rank circling the cuffs. Mason wondered whether this was to impress the pilot or whether Garner was always more formal in his dress when the ship was under way.

"All your men on board, sergeant?"

"All except one, sir."

"He'll be unlucky, then. We're leaving in ten minutes. Can't wait for him, you know. He'll have to join us at Southend."

Mason wondered whether Scarr would have the sense to do that if he found the ship had gone. It was more likely that he would go back home and stay there until he was routed out by the military police.

He went to the bulwark and scanned the river-side. The tide was high, and there was no mud showing, no sign of the ugly bits and pieces of jetsam that became visible when the river dropped away from its banks. There was no sign of Gunner Scarr either. Already two or three of the crew were on the forecastle, preparing to haul in the hawser as soon as it should be cast loose from the mooring-buoy. Steam was floating up from the winch, and from the funnel a rag of smoke was drifting lazily.

Mason crossed to the other side of the deck and saw a coaster much like the *Radgate* in build steaming past down-river. A gunner on the bridge lifted his hand in greeting and shouted some words that Mason failed to catch. He waved his own hand, returning the salutation, and moved away again restlessly.

At that moment Scarr appeared. His

head came up over the port bulwark, and a moment later he was standing on the deck.

Mason shouted: "Come here, you! Double!"

Scarr knew by the sound of the voice that this was not a moment to hesitate. He doubled.

"What in hell's this?" Mason said. "Do you call this eight o'clock? Do you call this getting back on time?" He was relieved that Scarr had turned up, but mixed with the relief was anger that Scarr should have given him so much anxiety. The anger spilled out in his voice.

Scarr shifted his feet, looked up at Mason, looked down at the deck, gave his lop-sided grin, and said: "Well, no, sarge; not exactly."

"Not exactly! You're damn right, not exactly. Not exactly by two hours. You're lucky to find the ship here at all." The winch on the forecastle began to draw the hawser in, rattling and steaming. "You hear that? That means we're about to leave. My God, you cut it fine." Because of the noise of the winch he had been forced to raise his voice; he was shouting at Scarr. "I suppose you've got an excuse."

"I'm sorry, sarge; straight, I am," Scarr said. "I didn't mean to let you down. And I wouldn't have done neither if it hadn't been for the accident."

"Let's have it," Mason said bleakly. "What accident?"

"The missus. Tripped on a mat and fell downstairs just as I was leaving. I had to go for the quack. I didn't know if she'd done herself an injury or something. Might have broken a bone, mightn't she? So that's how it is; what with one thing and another I couldn't get back time I should've been. You see how it is, don't you?"

"Good for the baby," Mason said grimly. He did not know how much of Scarr's tale to believe, even whether to believe any of it. The whole thing was probably a pack of lies from start to finish — the expected baby, the accident, going for the doctor — everything. But there was no way of checking up; there was no time. He had to accept the story.

He said: "You put me in a spot. I

didn't know whether you were going to turn up at all."

Scarr looked apologetic. "But it wasn't my fault, sarge. Circumstances beyond my control, as you might say. Besides, I didn't know the ship was leaving today. Anyway, here I am; so that's all right, ain't it? No bones broken."

"Is that what the doctor said?"

Scarr laughed appreciatively. "You will have your joke, won't you sarge? I'll say this for you — you've got a sense of humour, no two ways about it. What the doctor said! That's good, that is."

He glanced furtively at Mason, trying to gauge the extent of the sergeant's anger against him, the soothing effect of his explanation. "It's a worrying time for me, I can tell you. It'll be the first kid and all that. The first is always the most trouble, so they tell me."

The end of the hawser came up over the *Radgate*'s bows and she began to move out into mid-stream, her screw turning slowly over.

"You've got other worries now," Mason said. "We're going down to Southend. You know what that means. No more shore leave for you until after the invasion. You can concentrate on that for a time. I hope your wife isn't expecting you tonight."

He loaded the hope with sarcasm, testing Scarr's reaction, but the gunner appeared quite unmoved.

"Well, that's how it is, sarge. She'll have to get on without me, won't she?"

The *Radgate* dropped smoothly down-river, without fuss, without apparent exertion, negotiating the bends like a motorist on a road that he knows from long acquaintance. Tilbury and Gravesend slipped astern, and the river widened to the sea, the steel forts standing across the estuary like marine monsters with their feet in the mud and eyes all around their heads. A Thames barge crept out of the Medway, its great dark sail filling with the wind, and its hull so low in the water it seemed to have scarcely any freeboard at all. The *Radgate*'s anchor went down suddenly, the cable rattling through the hawse-pipe, red dust flying from the rusty links of the chain, and she came to rest with her stern pointing towards the sea.

"Nice weather for a seaside holiday," Gates said. "I remember when I used to come down to Southend with the old bucket and spade. Seems a long time ago now."

Scarr looked at him slyly. "It must have been. Didn't know you ever was a kid. Did you have a sailor suit?"

"Bet your life I did — with H.M.S. Victory in gold letters on the hatband. Never thought in those days I'd ever go to sea."

"I bet you was a nice little boy. I bet you had chubby knees."

"And what if I did? There's no harm in having chubby knees, is there?"

"I don't know," Scarr said. "I never had none." He changed the subject. "What you think we're stopping here for? To let the Old Man go ashore for a wet?"

"Use your loaf, boy. We've got to wait for a convoy, haven't we? You don't suppose we're going to slip round into the Channel all on our own. I thought you'd had some experience."

Scarr looked at the mass of shipping anchored in the estuary. "Seems like we

138

don't need to wait long. There's enough here for more than one convoy."

Mason went ashore in a naval auxiliary with Captain Garner; if the end of Southend Pier could be termed ashore. Southend still seemed to be about a mile away, and, coming in like this from the sea, the perspective was altered, so that you were inclined to look at the town far away in the distance as some kind of appendage to the pier, something that had grown on to its landward end like the bulb on the end of a glass tube; the pier was of first importance, the town secondary.

The weather had altered, become cool and cloudy. A wind slapped wavelets against the slimy piles of the pier, from which green fringes of seaweed hung like odorous curtains, lifting and falling with the lift and fall of the waves.

"The glass is dropping," Garner said. "We've missed the best of the weather, I'm thinking. Can't rely on it from one day to the next."

He climbed up the slippery ladder to the deck of the pier with the sure hand-and-foot action of the sailor. Mason followed, to find himself among the damp grey buildings, the silent turnstiles, the shuttered stalls.

"Ever been to Southend?" Garner asked.

"Never."

"Well, you'll be able to say you have now — technically."

There were gunlayers from other ships, naval and military, standing about in apathetic groups. A chief petty officer with brass-buttoned cuffs and a grating voice marshalled them into a room severely furnished with wooden forms and a blackboard — rather like a drab schoolroom. A lieutenant-commander, surveying his class gloomily through horn-rimmed glasses, proceeded to brief them for the coming operation. He pinned up a large drawing of a Typhoon, the underside of the wings marked in broad blue and white stripes.

"That is how our fighters will be marked. This time we're taking no chances. We don't want any more of that nonsense of shooting down our own planes. Anything with those wing markings you leave alone. Understand?"

A hoarse murmur that might have been no more than a clearing of throats indicated that they did understand.

"I hope you do." It was a pious hope, but the lieutenant-commander's whole manner seemed to indicate that he had in fact long since given up hoping for anything in the way of sense from the gunlayers of merchant vessels. He peered bleakly through his glasses at the men ranged in front of him. "If any of you is responsible for shooting down an Allied plane — " He left the sentence unfinished, but the threat was there.

A leading seaman said something about "Merchant Navy gunners, sir. Itchy trigger fingers — " and the lieutenant-commander rapped at him: "You're responsible; you men. You control the Merchant Navy gunners. That's your job. Is that clear?"

"Yes, sir." The leading-seaman sat down, his face red.

It was raining lightly when they went back to their ships; the naval auxiliary butting through the grey tidal waters that were neither Thames nor sea, but part one and part the other. Garner appeared gloomy, as though either the weather or the masters' conference which he had been attending had damped his spirits.

As they approached the *Radgate* Mason observed him gazing at his ship, and his face was set in a frown, the scar that years ago had twisted the contours of his mouth looking like a hinge to the upper lip. Mason wonderd what he was thinking. He followed the captain's gaze to the grey outline of the ship, which seemed to merge into the drizzle. There she was as her crew seldom saw her, like many another ship but having her own individuality for those whose home she was. What was the reason for Garner's frown? Was he thinking that this ship might soon be sunk, or did he see in her some measure of his own lack of success in life? Had he once had greater ambitions, the hope of becoming master of an ocean-going freighter, a smart tanker, or even a passenger liner? And was this what it had all come down to — middle age and the command of a rusting coaster?

He caught Mason looking at him, and said quickly: "You got your instructions?"

Mason held up a handful of papers; it was all down in black and white; they were not taking chances. "Down to the last detail, sir."

★ ★ ★

It was growing dusk when the ships drew up their anchors and moved into formation, heading out towards the sea. Earlier a naval craft had brought the *Radgate* a balloon, a miniature edition of those fat barrage-balloons that floated over London, but having solid fins, triangular in shape like the fins of sharks. This balloon now tugged at the ship's mast-head, its wire passing through a pulley on the mast and down to a winch on deck. Balloons were coastal convoy defences; you did not find them flying from the masts of ocean-going vessels. They were awkward things, inclined to leak, to become soft and flabby, to lose their fins, to perform weird gyrations, to nose-dive into the sea. But they were no doubt a deterrent to low-level air attacks, and at their worst they were far better than the canvas kites that had once been tried in a similar rôle.

Mason had set his gun watches — Scarr and Rickman on the port Oerlikon, himself and Gates on the starboard one, and the two naval ratings on the twin. It would be four hours on and four off, turn and turn about. For himself, sleeping in the chart-room was now out of the question, but he had arranged to use Gates's bunk; when he was off watch Gates would be on, so the arrangement ought to work satisfactorily. He gave Gates the evening watch, and relieved him at midnight. Scarr was then on the port gun. He had worked it out like that so that he might have some control over Scarr. He felt that he could rely on Gates and Rickman, and also on Sims and Vickers; but he did not trust Scarr.

At twelve o'clock it was a dark, thick night — chilly too. Mason wrapped himself up well in duffel coat, scarf, and woollen cap, and went across to the firemen's fo'c'sle to make sure that Scarr was stirring. Rather to his surprise, he found him just coming out on deck. Perhaps, Mason thought, he had misjudged the fellow, or perhaps Scarr

144

was just keeping on the right side of the sergeant after having already blotted his copybook.

He seemed perky, apparently not letting any worries about his expectant wife cast him down. "Okay, sarge; here I am. Didn't think I'd be late again, did you?"

"I wasn't too sure. Have you had any sleep?"

"Not me. I been playing pontoon with some of the boys. Won a bit an' all. Just as well it was time to come on watch. Me luck might've changed."

Mason groped his way towards the bridge, stepping warily in the darkness. Scarr followed him closely.

"Nice night, sarge. Hope it don't turn to rain. Still, you want it black when you're going through the Strait. They got some nasty old guns on the French coast. Don't want any of them banging away at us."

Mason found Gates in the starboard gun-box. "Anything exciting happened?"

Gates, who had been sheltering from the wind in the lee of the Oerlikon, moved out to allow Mason to take his place. "Nothing. Got a bit close to the tail of the ship in front once or twice,but no contact. Been some sparks from the funnel. Look; there she goes again."

Looking aft, Mason could see a line of sparks shooting upward like the trail of a rocket, startlingly vivid against the dark background of the night.

"They ought to do something about that," Gates said. "But I don't suppose they will. Don't seem to worry about little things like that on board this ship. There's the Old Man lighting his pipe in the wheelhouse now — no more concern for black-out regulations than if he was in the middle of the Gobi desert.

Mason saw the flare of the match in the wheelhouse lighting up the windows. He could see Garner's head illuminated as the flame dipped and jumped to the sucking of his pipe. The match showed up the helmsman and the interior of the wheelhouse, but Garner, engrossed in the lighting of his pipe, seemed perfectly oblivious of the brilliance of his fireworks. Then the match went out, and all that was left was a small red glow that came and went, and the strong odour of tobacco-smoke.

"That's a damn-fool thing to do," Mason said. "Doesn't he realize how far that light could show?" He felt inclined to go into the wheelhouse and tell Garner off. But he realized that this would do no good. Garner was captain; he was the law on board this ship. "Is this the practice in coasters?" he asked. "He'd be liable to be shot at if he lit up like that in a deep-sea convoy. It's as good as a signal."

"I wouldn't call it general," Gates said. "Some of 'em are as strict as you'd want; but there's some that are pretty lax. Maybe they just don't think."

Mason was about to make another remark, but Gates had gone, sinking into the darkness like a shadow. Mason gazed over the starboard side, where the invisible coast of England was sliding past. Behind him was France, waiting for the invasion, and he did not yet know when or where that invasion would take place.

★ ★ ★

The *Radgate* came to anchor in the Solent — a Solent packed with almost every type and size of vessel — freighters, coasters, landing-craft, motor launches — a regular shipbuilder's exhibition. Small boats, and others not so small, were chuffing to and fro, moving from one ship to another on apparently urgent and endless business, filling the air with the sound of their engines, and cutting short-lived ribbons of white foam out of the ruffled surface of the water.

The Isle of Wight looked pleasant and peaceful, no more than half a mile away. It looked as if it could not really concern itself with the fuss and preparation for war that was going on all around it, as if this were not truly its business, and it were simply waiting for the tall-masted, white-sailed yachts to come back like swans that had migrated, sweeping up the Channel with canvas billowing and bones in their teeth.

The crew were rigging a tarpaulin over a derrick boom that stretched across the forward hatch. They fastened it down on either side of the coaming to form a rough tent with the boom as a ridge-pole.

"What's that in aid of?" Mason asked one of the seamen.

"For the troops."

"What troops?"

"You'll see."

The troops arrived on the following day — a docks-operating unit of the Royal Engineers — fifty men complete with kit, swarming on board the little ship. The tent erected on the hatch was for them; it was to be their home until they were disembarked in France; there they were to sleep, bedded above the high-explosive ammunition which it was to be their task to unload. It was a case of taking your dockers with you.

"Nice stuff to sleep on," Gates said. "Proper feather-bed."

"Safe enough," Scarr said. "Safe as houses if we don't get a shell or a bomb or a torpedo into us, or if we don't hit a flaming mine. Then we'll all go up. Nobody'll know much about it."

The major in command of the soldier-dockers was a big, tough-looking man who, so one of the corporals told Mason, had once been a Liverpool stevedore. He sounded like it. He was democratic enough to play cards with his men and take their money without rancour. They addressed him off-duty as Sid, and he would swear at a man one minute and clap him on the shoulder the next. Mason had seen nothing like it since his contact with American troops on board the *Mauretania*. Superficially it seemed that all discipline had gone, thrown overboard with the garbage; that it had given way to a happy-go-lucky, come-as-you-please attitude of each man for himself. But this was not so. There was a time for play and a time for work, and Mason never heard the major give an order that was not instantly obeyed. The men might call him Sid, but they knew that Sid was the boss.

With these fifty extra men on board the *Radgate* was as crowded as a pleasure-steamer. And there was nothing for them to do but sit on the hatches, lean on the bulwarks, smoke and talk and wait.

"It'll be a damned good job to get it over and done with," Scarr grumbled, "if only so's we can get a bit of deck space to ourselves again."

Scarr was feeling sore. He had joined

in a poker school, and had been skinned. Therefore he was inclined to look upon all sappers with a peculiarly jaundiced eye.

Mason too was eager to go. This waiting about simply played on the nerves. You could not tell what was coming, what it would be like; so you imagined things. You wondered whether it was right that the Germans had ways of setting the sea on fire, secret weapons that would blast an invading force out of the water; you could not entirely free your mind of such ideas, however much you might try to do so. Therefore it would be better to get it over and have done with it, to know the worst. And the sooner the invasion took place the sooner would the War be over; and the back to Civvie Street, to the farm — and Clare?

When Mason's thoughts reached this point he was brought up with a jerk. Between Clare and himself there was now another figure — Jo. Being honest with himself, he had to admit that it was to Jo that he longed to go back. He wondered what she might be doing at that moment, and, knowing so little

151

about her, his mind was plagued with jealousy; he was jealous of anyone who might be looking at her, speaking to her, laughing with her.

Telling himself that he was a fool made no difference. Fool or not, he wanted her; he wanted to have her always. The thought that he might never see her again was unacceptable. Whatever happened he would go back to her. And if she had disappeared, gone away, he would search through the whole of London, the whole world if necessary, and he would find her. But there was no reason to suppose that she would have disappeared. No reason why she should not still be in the old house when he returned. If he returned.

The 4th of June was a dull, cold day with rain and wind. And the 5th had been fixed for the invasion of France — D-day. They all knew that now. They were all prepared.

"Tomorrow," Gates said, "we'll be away. Tomorrow we'll know what it's like going back. It's been a long time since Dunkirk, the hell of a long time."

Mason looked at him, a thought

suddenly entering his head. "Were you at Dunkirk too?"

Gates noded. "I got away on the fourth day. A stockbroker with a motor-cruiser took me off with about thirty others — nearly swamped the damned thing. You know how it was — bombs falling — hell and all of noise; and this stockbroker, he must have been nearly sixty and fatter than I am, he just said, cool as you like: 'If they sink my boat it's going to cost the insurance company two thousand pounds.' I never heard whether they did sink it. I often wondered what happened to him after he got shot of us. He was wearing the old school tie and a bowler hat and I don't think he'd shaved for three days — nor slept, neither, by the look of him."

"I got away by the Mole," Mason said. "In a destroyer. The destroyer bought it next time out. I was lucky. A whole lot of us were lucky. It doesn't pay to trust to that sort of luck too often."

This was something else he had not known about Gates. Dunkirk, the Russia run — these experiences they had shared. There is a bond between men who have faced the same dangers, who have looked together into the face of death. Mason felt his heart warm towards Gates.

Curious, he asked: "Why haven't you had a stripe? Have you never been put in for one?"

Gates smiled. "I thought you knew. I *was* a sergeant."

"They stripped you? What for?" he regretted the question almost immediately. It was not always tactful to ask a man how he had come to lose his rank. Perhaps it was better not to know. Perhaps Gates would refuse to tell him. But if he did Mason knew he would for ever be wondering why those stripes were lost, and what blemish there was on Gates's character. "You don't have to tell me," he said.

Gates noticed Mason's discomfiture, but was himself unconcerned. "Don't let it bother you; I'm happy as a gunner as I ever was as a sergeant. But the cause of my downfall was smuggling."

"Oh, that." Mason was relieved. He wanted to be able to respect Gates, and he had been afraid of hearing something so discreditable that it would have made respect impossible. But smuggling — that was nothing. If everyone who had smuggled cigarettes and silk stockings and watches into the country had been found out there would have been a dearth of N.C.O.'s in the Maritime Regiment of the Royal Artillery.

"What was it?" he asked,

"Bicycle tyres from Ireland. They were stuffed in a kitbag. I'd done it before. But a fool of a gunner threw the kitbag down from the ship to the quay in Glasgow. Sarge, I give you my word I thought it was going to bounce all the way to Sauchiehall Street; but what it did was bounce on to the great big feet of a copper. I suppose coppers are just naturally suspicious or something. Anyway, this one seemed to think there was some peculiarity about a bouncing kitbag. So he looked inside, and that was that. I lost twenty quid's worth of tyres and three stripes, all in one go. I was sorry about the tyres."

Mason went up to the chart-room, thinking he might start on that letter to Phil Brightwell. Burma seemed the hell of a long way off. It was a different kind of war over there, a war in which the Japs were not the only enemies; you had also to contend with the jungle, the heat, the insects, the rain, the leeches. Mason was glad he had got himself into the Maritime Regiment. The sea was better than the jungle or the desert.

He did not write the letter, because he found Captain Garner and the mate poring over some charts on the table. They were so absorbed in what they were studying that they did not even look up when Mason looked in at the doorway. Only Cerberus, stretched out on the settee, lifted his head and gazed at Mason, opened his jaws in a long yawn, and went to sleep again.

Mason went out of the wheel house and examined the port Oerlikon, the gun for which Scarr and Rickman were responsible. To his satisfaction, he found that it was now in first-class order. He wondered what it would have been like if Bombardier Betts had still been in charge. He wondered where Betts was now, whether he was missing the invasion. He leaned on the edge of the gun-box and looked round at all the ships in the anchorage, wondering in how many of them were friends of his, men he had sailed with to distant countries, men with whom he had faced the dangers of torpedo and bomb and mine, men who were now going on the greatest land and sea operation of all time.

He heard the captain and mate come out of the wheelhouse, and he watched them, two squat, solid men, going down the bridge ladder. All the ship's officers were short; there was not a tall man among them. Perhaps they were of a special breed designed for small ships, designed to fit into tiny cabins, low doorways, truncated bunks. Yet what they lacked in height they seemed to make up in width; there was plenty of meat there, even if it did appear to have been shaken down in the sack.

The chart-room was reeking of pipe-smoke when Mason went into it. Cerberus had followed his master, but the indent of his body was there in the settee with a few loose hairs as the mark of his former presence. The charts were still on the table, and Mason examined them. They told him very little; he could not identify any coastline.

He switched on the metal-cased radio receiver and twiddled the dials. The set crackled; Morse signals stammered out of the loudspeaker; the sound of music — jazz — came very faintly; it was like hearing a band playing behind the closed doors of a ballroom. Mason switched the set off, pushed the charts to one side, and fished his leather writing-wallet out of the kitbag standing in a corner of the room.

He had intended writing that letter to Phil, and perhaps one to Clare also, but when his pen moved on the paper it was to Jo that he wrote. He knew that he would never send the letter; and for that reason he could make it completely honest. He could tell her how much a part of his life she had become. She was like a star-shell that had blazed suddenly in front of his eyes, blinding him, blacking out all other light. It was not three days since he had first seen her, and in those three days she had altered his whole outlook. 'Jo, darling; I want you to know . . . '

The words poured out on to the paper, but when he read them through they semed like gibberish. He stared at them, then crumpled the paper in his hand and went out to the leeward side of the bridge. He flung the ball of paper away over the side; the wind caught it and carried it in a long, shallow flight to the water. Mason could see it bobbing about on the surface like a ping-pong ball on a jet in a shooting-gallery. He watched it until it disappeared.

He turned then and looked down at the foredeck where the soldiers were moving, restless with expectation. Everywhere there was expectation, the sensation of something really big about to happen, something which had been in people's minds for years, continually demanded, continually postponed. Mason thought of the words he had so often seen scrawled in chalk or paint on walls and hoardings: 'Invade in the west now.' For years there had been those parrot-cries demanding a Second Front, echoing Stalin.

He wondered with a certain bitterness how many of those who so bravely chalked up the slogans, who talked so airily of throwing an army ashore on the coast of France, would go with that army, would face the machine-guns and flame-throwers, the mortars and the cannon. It was easy to mouth the word invasion; it was not so easy nor so pleasant to spill your blood and bowels in making the word a reality. To speak of flinging an army ashore as though it were no more difficult an operation than flinging a cricket-ball! Madness! But the whole world was mad. What brains, what endeavour had gone to the mounting of this invasion! What thousands would die before it was complete! It was all madness.

It was now hours to sailing time. Two more hours and they would be away. The soldiers congealed into little groups talking, smoking, playing cards; and the ship's cat, moving disdainfully among them, seemed to resent the presence of so much humanity. The cook, unshaven, a hand-rolled cigarette adhering to his lower lip like some obscene growth, dealt out Spam and biscuits as though conferring a favour; and the chief engineer, encountering the mate amidships, turned his back on him and retraced his steps, wanting no more contact with that man so similar in appearance to himself than was to be had through the tenuous medium of a speaking-tube.

The Solent, grey and cold under the cold grey sky, was restless also. The wind troubled it, roughening the surface of the water and sending little jets of spume from the white caps of the wavelets. The ships tugged at their cables, swinging with the tide.

Rickman, leaning over the starboard side, said: "Here's another launch coming. What's it this time?"

"More orders," Mason said. The launch was moving fast, cutting its white path towards the *Radgate*. As it drew level a voice shouted hoarsely: "Invasion postponed twenty-four hours. Postponed twenty-four hours."

Then the launch had swept past and was on its way to the next ship and the next, giving each the brief news that it was to be the 6th and not the 5th of June.

And the tension went out of the ship

like a breath. They felt like runners who have been keyed up for the start of a race and then are told that it is not to take place until the following day. There was a sense of let-down, of anti-climax, of being cheated. It would have been better to have gone.

"Twenty-four hours," Rickman said. "What can you do with twenty-four hours?"

"You can sleep," Gates said.

6

The 6th of June

THE corvette was moving slowly, leading the way through the swept channel with the *Radgate* following. The gap between the two ships began to close. Mason from the wing of the bridge could see that they were overhauling the warship. Then a loud-hailer on the corvette was trained aft and a voice very clearly, very calmly, said: "*Radgate* ahoy! If you do not keep in position and moderate your confounded speed you'll blow yourself to hell — and me also."

The *Radgate* slackened speed and dropped astern.

It was a bright, clear morning with high clouds, the sun warm on the ships, reflected in the blue water off the Normandy coast. Through the night the *Radgate* had steamed across Channel with the sappers sleeping on her tented hatches; all night in company with an armada visible only as dark shapes ahead and astern, an armada that as day broke over a flat sea became recognizable as a floating bridge of ships and landing-craft stretching in a long line from one horizon to the other, and moving steadily, inexorably forward.

Overhead the aircraft swept by in waves like hosts of gigantic birds, filling the air with the thunder of their engines. In the distance the first rumble of explosions, the bombs and the guns, was audible. The Second Front, so long demanded, so long awaited, had opened at last.

The light was strengthening as the corvette led them in, threading the narrow channel that the minesweepers had cleared. They went slowly to avoid detonating acoustic mines; they kept carefully to the marked channel, straying neither to starboard not to port, conscious always of the cargo of high explosive stowed away in the holds. They came to the position that had been allotted to them and dropped anchor.

"We're here," Mason said. "This is it."

He stood on one side of the Oerlikon with Gates on the other and looked towards the land. It was clearly visible now as the sun rose — the beaches of Arromanches where the blood was still fresh in the soft sand, where the wire was tangled and the pill-boxes blasted open. Looking across the shimmering water, he wondered whether Gates was also thinking of another French beach that had been soaked with blood four years ago. It had been so different then — different in everything except the blood.

How many already? he wondered. How many who yesterday had been alive and young would not see today's sunset; how many had known only that mad rush from the steel jaws of the assault craft, the splashing of salt water about their legs, the gasping agony of running up the beach with the soft sand clogging their steps as in a nightmare, and then the bullet and nothing more. Months of training, months of preparation, and in two minutes the War was over — a bullet in the brain and sand choking the mouth, sand becoming redder and redder, and the eyes blind, the ears deaf — no more taste, no more feeling, no more fear.

Mason experienced a feeling almost of guilt, standing on the bridge of this ship that had moved in so easily, without resistance from a Luftwaffe rendered innocuous by the overwhelming superiority of the Allied air forces. He felt that he ought to be ashore, taking part in the real work, instead of standing by and watching from the comparative safety of a ship's deck. He had been one of those driven out from Dunkirk; now some one else was doing the job of breaking back into the fortress of Europe. He felt as though he personally had laid that task which should have been his own on those other shoulders.

It was obvious that Gates had no such qualms. "Sooner them than me," he said.

They could see the houses a little way back from the shore, houses fortified by the Germans. Tracers, like balls of fire, were probing into them. One house began to burn, the smoke of its destruction going straight up in the still air. Two landing-craft with 3-inch guns mounted on them moved up to the beach and began firing at the houses. Pieces were chipped away from the walls, a chimney fell in a cloud of dust and rubble. More assault-craft spouted men on to the beach, and they ran forward, crouching, as though the loads on their backs prevented them from standing upright. Some fell and did not get up.

The noise of the battle was confused, deadened by distance. Bursts of machine-gun fire, the thud of mortars, the angry crack of the bigger guns: it added up to no complete symphony, no rounded, masterly composition, but a collection of individual performances bursting out in sudden anger, sudden jubilation, or sudden fear. In it all the human voice was lost, overwhelmed, like that of a weak singer in a Wagnerian opera.

"I wonder whether they'll hold it," Gates said. "You put your foot in the door. Then you've got to make sure it ain't cut off. Those boys are having a tough time of it. Sooner them than me. My God, yes; sooner them than me a thousand bloody times."

From the distance there was an air

of unreality about it all. It was like looking at a play through the wrong end of a telescope. The men on the shore were puppets; you had difficulty in appreciating them as human beings, men with blood to shed, eyes to be blinded, arms to lose, bowels to be gashed and torn by steel. The puppets swarmed up the beaches, dug little holes for themselves in the sand, carried guns, drove tanks, hauled, sweated, panted, cursed, trembled, and died. And yet, standing off there in the morning sunshine, it was all as unreal as something flashed upon a screen; it was as though whenever you tired of it you could leave your seat and go away and forget.

"Did you ever see so many ships?" Gates said. "I never did."

They lay on the water like insects on the surface of a pond, some moving, some at anchor; ships in their scores, their hundreds, with the landing-craft and the amphibians going back and forth, ferrying men and material from ship to shore. This was a landing in force; such force as had never been seen before and was never likely to be seen again.

A battleship to seaward of the *Radgate* began to fire its 14-inch guns, throwing shells far inland. The slam of the heavy guns shook the windows in the wheelhouse, and the shells went overhead with a rushing sound like express-trains moving through the air.

"I'd rather be on the tail-end of those little presents than on the other," Gates said. "They'll make a hole somewhere."

The hatch-covers were off. They had in fact been off long before the ship came to anchor. The derricks were rigged. The sappers were on the job now, helped by the *Radgate*'s crew. Winches clattered, slings came swinging up out of the holds with small-arms ammunition and drums of petrol. A landing-craft eased its rectangular shape alongside and was made fast; the derrick booms swung overboard; the slings were lowered, emptied, drawn up again.

The sea was not completely flat; there was a slight swell, and the landing-craft lifted and fell, lifted and fell, with a rhythmic, hypnotic motion. Some of the sappers who had gone over the side to unload the slings were sick. Mason could see them running to the side of the landing-craft to vomit. He did not envy them. The work had to go on.

It was while he was watching the unloading that he first heard the high, thin whine of shells, and saw splashes between the ship and the beach. Some shore battery must have opened up; he wondered how long they would take to find the range. He had plenty of time for wondering; there was nothing else for him to do but stand by the Oerlikon and watch for enemy planes that did not come.

He saw another shell drop in the sea, but it was impossible to tell whether the guns were firing to any system or whether the shells were simply being lobbed seaward in the hope that they might, in that mass of shipping, find some target. Away on the left, towards what must surely be the mouth of the Orne, somebody was putting up a smoke-screen; it was like a white mist drifting across the water. Ashore the initial ferocity had died away, leaving only a sporadic outburst as pockets of resistance were mopped up. The main battle had moved inland, the tanks and infantry thrusting forward and fanning out to form and hold the bridgehead through which supplies and men and yet more men could come.

After a while the shelling from the shore battery ceased, and Mason was not sorry that this should be so. He did not believe that the men working on the cargo had noticed the shells; they were too busy. The ones who were being sick did not care.

The landing-craft moved away towards the beach and another came out and took its place; then another and another.

The day wore on. A great fleet of aircraft and gliders passed overhead. From beyond the perimeter of the bridgehead a curtain of fire went up to meet them. The tugs loosed their gliders and turned, heading seaward. The gliders drifted down and disappeared from sight beyond the rise of the land. And again Mason had the impression of unreality. The gliders were just so many paper darts, and their tugs, the Stirlings and Halifaxes, though they might have gashes in their wings as they came away, though they might have dead engines here and there, were not real either. Nothing was real except the sappers being sick and the winches clattering.

"I wouldn't have missed it," Gates said. "Not for anything I wouldn't."

★ ★ ★

When darkness came the work on the cargo ceased. Mason went up to the starboard Oerlikon to relieve Gates.

"Get yourself some sleep. You may be needed up here again before long."

Gates went down the bridge ladder and Mason leaned on the side of the gun-box. A queer, unnatural hush had settled on the anchorage, a hush that seemed to be accentuated by the occasional sound of a motor-launch. From the shore Mason could hear the sound of gunfire, rumbling sullenly in the distance. He could see the flashes of the guns like summer lightning, and here and there a flame leaping up.

The night was cool and still. On the deck below the weary sappers were taking what sleep they could before their work should begin again with the coming of dawn. And what was happening ashore? How far inland had the invading forces thrust their way? When would the counter-attack come? Could they hold off that counter-attack? These were the questions that only time could answer.

Suddenly Mason heard the faint sound of a violin and of a man singing in a deep bass. The song was that most beautiful and nostaglic of all sea shanties, *Shenandoah*. 'Oh, Shenandoah, I love your daughter . . . ' Mason thought he recognized the voice as that of Mawby, the chief engineer; he was probably sitting in Garner's cabin singing to the accompaniment of Garner's violin.

Mason wondered what the mate thought of the singing, but he did not have to wonder long, for at that moment Gregory himself came out on to the starboard wing of the bridge, a dark, massive shape in the dim light of the stars.

"Damned caterwauling," Gregory said. "Enough to turn a man's stomach — truth, it is."

Mason could see the mate's face turned

towards him, a pale oval. "Is that the sergeant?"

"Yes, sir."

"What do you think of that damned noise?"

Mason was tactful. "I've heard better singing."

"Damn right you have. Why don't they go to sleep or play cards or something?" He was stamping backward and forward on the meagre space of bridge, and Mason formed the opinion that Mr Gregory was just the least bit on edge, nervy.

His next words strengthened the impression. "What's your view of things, sergeant? Do you think Jerry will try a night raid? He's got all these ships gathered here in a lump. Couldn't ask for a better target. What do you say?"

"He may try it if he's got the planes."

"Can't have lost 'em all, can he? Stands to reason he'll have some in hand for a job like this. He knew it was coming. He'd be prepared." Gregory was peering into the darkness, as if trying to see into the enemy's mind. From below came the sound of another song

174

succeeding *Shenandoah*. It had a quicker tempo: *Camptown Races*.

"Oh, damn and blast them!" Gregory muttered. "Damn and blast their bloody eyes! Why in hell don't they go to sleep?" He rested his hands on the rail of the bridge, and Mason judged that he was looking down on the foredeck. He seemed to be reeling off a list of the cargo that was still in the hold, ticking off the items in a low voice: "Petrol, small-arms ammo, 4.5 inch shells, cordite, detonators . . . " It was as though he were reckoning up the extent of the damage a bomb could do. But after a while he went back into the wheelhouse and Mason was left to himself.

It was some time later when the first plane came over dropping parachute flares. Mason could hear the heavy droning of the engines, and then the flares came dropping slowly, lighting up the ships and reflected garishly in the water. Gregory reappeared from the wheelhouse, his face like the bright red face of a devil in the light of the flares.

"That's it. That's the start. He'll be bombing next. What you going to do?"

"Nothing — yet. Nothing I can do."

"You can fire at that plane, can't you?"

"Not much use firing at something you can't see."

"You can hear it."

"Firing at sound is a waste of ammunition."

"At the flares, then. For God's sake, you've got to do something."

"Mr Gregory," Mason said, "I don't interfere with your job. I wish you'd leave me to look after mine."

The mate, perhaps conscious that he had been allowing his nervousness to become too apparent, took a grip on himself and spoke more quietly. "All right, sergeant; I suppose you know best. But there's other ships firing. Look at the tracer."

The tracer was criss-crossing in bright arcs of fire, and some of the arcs had very low trajectories. Mason guessed that most of the guns were firing at the slowly descending parachute flares. It was more than a waste of ammunition; it was a danger to other ships.

"They're damn fools," he said. He had

not heard any bombs falling, but soon there must surely be some. He had a feeling of nakedness in that bright red light. It was like being on a stage bathed in limelight and waiting for some one, invisible in the dark auditorium, to start throwing things. The trouble was that on this particular stage there were no wings into which the actors could run for shelter; it was a stage to which you were firmly anchored, from which you could not move.

Gates appeared suddenly, slipping into the narrow box to take his place beside the gun.

"What woke you?" Mason asked.

"I haven't been to sleep," Gates said. "I thought I heard a Jerry plane, so I got up and saw the flares. Nice sample of light, and no mistake. You wouldn't think they could hang in the air all that time, would you?"

The flares dropped very slowly, but even when they reached the water they were not finished; they appeared to burst into new life, floating on the surface like little fire-ships, brilliant jewels of light in a dark world.

Again there came the drone of aeroengines overhead, then the whistle of falling bombs. The *Radgate* vibrated to some shock-wave passing through the water. It was as though a gigantic hand had grasped the keel, had shaken it, and then let go.

"I don't think they hit anything," Gates said. "You know, sarge, this is not nice, not nice at all — just standing up there and waiting for something to hit us. You don't think we ought to let fly a bit?"

"Just blind away into the air regardless? There'd be some sense in that. I thought you knew better."

"Well, of course, I know it wouldn't really do any good. But somehow you don't feel so bad when the old gun is blasting away. But, of course, there's no sense in it."

"You're as bad as the mate. He was out here a minute ago, wanting me to blaze away at the flares."

"Jittery, is he?"

"Seemed a bit on edge. I shouldn't have expected him to be. He doesn't look the type."

"You can't tell." Gates cocked his head on one side, listening. "What's that? Don't sound like another plane — not exactly."

"Motor-launch, I'd say. Look, there it is; over there. Seems to be smoking."

"That's it," Gates said. "Not a bad idea either. There's a hell of a lot too much light around the place. A bit of smoke is just what the doctor ordered."

The launch swept past, white vapour pouring from its stern; farther off another one could be dimly seen. The vapour drifted around the ships like a fog. It rolled over the *Radgate*, ghostly, enveloping. Mason's nose tingled as he breathed it in. It had a stinging quality; he could feel it probing the tiny cuts in his face where earlier the razor had nicked his skin.

"Hope it ain't poisonous," Gates said, coughing.

"Hardly likely."

"Unless those launches are Jerry ones. That'd be a how-do-you-do, wouldn't it? Gas the whole blooming invasion fleet."

"You're feeling all right, aren't you?"

"I don't know. I'll tell you in the

morning — if I'm still alive and kicking."

"You will be."

The flares spluttered and died; the light faded; the sound of the launches died away, and the night became once again dark and silent. On the deck below a man cried out suddenly in his sleep. The anchor-chain groaned in the hawse-pipe as the ship swung round with the tide.

"You might as well go and get your head down," Mason said. "You'll be needing all the sleep you can get before this show is finished."

Gates said: "I'd rather be up here. I'll just wedge myself in a corner and take forty winks."

Mason could hear him making himself as comfortable as possible on the floor of the gun-box. In a few minutes his steady breathing showed that he had fallen asleep.

Mason leaned against the gun pedestal and thought of Jo. Would she, he wondered, be thinking of him? He was pretty sure when he had told her that he would not be back for a week or two that she had guessed where he was going.

Now the news of the invasion would be splashing the papers, jamming the ether, providing conversation in pub and shop and café. And Jo would know where he was; he was sure of it. And, knowing, would she worry? If he failed to come back, would she care? Would it mean anything to her beyond a momentary regret?

He believed it would. He believed that, though they had spent no more than a few all too brief hours together, she loved him as deeply as he loved her. He had seen it in her eyes that morning when he had gone away; he had seen the pain there that had not been there before.

Their meeting had been like the clash of two elements which cannot touch without coalescing, compelled by some attraction not to be resisted. He did not want to resist it. He wanted to take all that Jo could give. When he was with her he could think of nothing else; nothing else seemed to matter. He was in a kind of dream from which he had no desire to be awakened. That was why he no longer wished to know anything more about her than he could see with his own eyes, touch with is own hands, taste with his own lips. That was enough.

He was still thinking of Jo when the next parachute flares began to fall. He looked up and saw one hanging like a great red star almost immediately above the ship. Gates woke with a start and got up. And at that moment the port Oerlikon started firing, its tracers leaping up towards the flare.

Mason went through the wheelhouse fast — out on to the port wing of the bridge. He brushed past a dark, lumpy shape that he guessed was the mate, and then his hand was grasping Scarr's shoulder, his voice snarling in Scarr's ear.

"Stop that, you bloody fool!"

Scarr's finger slackened on the trigger bar and the gun stopped vibrating. Suddenly everything seemed very silent; only the drone of the aircraft overhead serving to break that silence.

"What in hell do you think you're playing at?"

Scarr lay back in the harness of the Oerlikon gun, twisting round to look into Mason's face, his own appearing like that of some small demon on the light of the flare.

"What were you firing at, for God's sake?"

Scarr pointed upward. "At that."

"That flare? You wouldn't hit it in a thousand years. Who told you to fire?"

"The mate, sarge, Mr Gregory. He told me to. I thought it was all right if he told me."

"It wasn't all right; it was all wrong. And you'll take your orders from me. Wait till you see me fire. Is that clear?" Scarr muttered sulkily: "Clear enough."

"Right, then."

Mason went back to the starboard side without troubling to speak to Mr Gregory. Damned fool, interfering! Why didn't he stick to his own job?

"There's one coming in now," Gates said. "Listen!" It's a lot lower."

Mason listened. This plane was certainly very much lower than the other. It might, of course be the same one returning to bomb the targets illuminated by the flares. The engine-note increased in volume. Mason strapped himself into the harness of the Oerlikon, the semicircular shoulder pads resting on this shoulders. He swung the gun-barrel round in the direction of the noise, trying to see beyond the radius of the flares, out into the darkness.

Then he heard the whistle of the bombs, and wanted instinctively to duck down behind the wall of the gun-box. He did in fact dip his head, but then, feeling the strap at his back, he regained his self-control The bombs could not have been really close; they caused only a small vibration in the *Radgate*; but the plane that had dropped them appeared suddenly as a shadowy silhouette low down on the starboard side. Mason began firing just as a dozen other guns in other ships opened up.

The plane had appeared only for a moment, and then was gone, slipping into the darkness beyond the garish light of the flares. Mason stoped firing.

He had not fired enough to empty the magazine; he had used perhaps half of the sixty rounds that had been in it. Nevertheless, he thought it might be a good idea to replace it with a full one. He put the safety-catch to 'Safe,' and with his right hand pushed forward the lever of the magazine-catch.

"Change."

Gates lifted the half-empty magazine off the gun and put a full on in its place.

"Okay."

The glow from the flares was dying again, the stark outlines of the ships merging slowly into the background of the darkness.

"We could do with another smoke-screen," Gates said. "That plane is still hanging around. Maybe more than one."

The sound of the engines was still clearly audible, but it was difficult to distinguish between planes and launches at a distance. Mason heard the mate's voice behind him.

"Do you think you hit him?"

He answered impatiently: "Not much chance — firing at a shadow." Not only firing at a shadow, but blinded by the flash of the gun, so that after the first round you simply had to trust to luck. Anti-aircraft fire was a haphazard game at night; you would have to be supremely lucky to score a hit.

The mate said: "Well, I am glad you

had a go." There was more warmth in his voice. Mason felt that he had raised himself in Mr Gregory's estimation, even if he had accomplished nothing else by his firing.

"Here comes another one," Gates said.

Mason swung the gun round, his feet stumbling on the floor of the gun-box. The plane seemed to be coming in from beyond the bows of the ship, the note of the engines gradually rising in pitch like a warning. Mason peered into the darkness, trying to discover some outline, some moving shadow that he might identify as a target. He heard Gates mutter, "Can't see a thing, not a damn thing," and then suddenly a brilliant white light appeared in the sky, like a lamp suspended in mid-air. The German plane had switched on a searchlight.

Its beam, like a long white finger, probed for the ships, found one ahead of the *Radgate*, and held it glowingly illumined. The ship was a big freighter. Mason had examined it in daylight — a Liberty ship of some 7000 tons. He had noticed then that the ship had a Bofors gun; and it was that gun which now began to talk. Mason could see the tracers moving the sky like red balls drawn up on a string.

"They'll have him," Gates said. "They can't miss if they ain't blind."

It was, in fact, the easiest of targets. The plane was apparently diving on the ship, and with the searchlight shining like a baleful eye the gunners had nothing to do but fire up into that eye.

Mason brought his own gun to bear and pressed the trigger. He fired one burst, then another, and another. He saw a streak of flame shoot suddenly from a point just to one side of the searchlight. The light went out, and then the whole plane was visible, flickeringly illuminated by the crimson flare of the burning engine.

It seemed very low, little more than mast-height. It pulled out of its dive and swept away from the Liberty ship with the bright rags of flame trailing from its starboard wing. It levelled and came towards the *Radgate*, one engine on fire, the other roaring.

Mason pumped more shells at it until the gun would fire no more, the magazine empty. He pushed the catch forward with his finger-tips and yelled to Gates: "Change!" But he knew that there would be no time to fire any more rounds at that particular plane; that there would be no need to do so.

He thought for a moment that the bomber was going to fall on the *Radgate*; it was coming towards the ship with the starboard engine trailing its banner of flame, and it was falling rapidly. Gates slammed the full magazine into place, looked round, and saw the plane. He gave a yelp like a dog that somebody has stood on; just the one yelp and nothing more. Then he stood perfectly rigid, perfectly silent, waiting.

Mason's brain worked very clearly in those few moments that he was sure were to be his last moments of life. The *Radgate*'s holds contained drums of petrol and high-explosive ammunition; a burning plane, perhaps with bombs still in its racks, was about to fall on her. There could be only one result of that impact — a shattering explosion that would blow the whole ship apart, scatter it in pieces all about the anchorage. In that moment he did not feel particularly afraid; there seemed to be no time for fear. His emotion was rather one of regret — regret that he should have to go now when there was still so much left to do, so many tasks left uncompleted, so many paths unexplored, so many puzzles unsolved, so many delights untasted.

Perhaps all men felt the same in the instant of death if they had time to feel anything; perhaps all experienced that sudden wave of anger, driving out fear; anger at the abruptness, at the sharp knife severing everything in one swift, unforgiving blow. If there could only have been another year, another month, a week, a day, even a single hour — so much could have been done to sort things out, to prepare for the final journey.

Mason looked at the plane and thought: I shall never see Jo again, and she will never know what happened to me. It was the fact that she would not know that worried him. Some people were suppose to have felt the death of a loved one far away in the instant of that death. Mason did not know whether there was any truth in the story, but he had a sudden picture of Jo waking in the night and sitting up in bed and crying out. He could even hear her crying, crying . . .

But in fact it was Gates shouting in his ear. And he realized that he was not going to die after all — not yet. For the plane had swerved away to port, dipping its wing. The nose came up, as though in a last desperate attempt to gain height, and then, just as it appeared almost to have cleared the *Radgate*, it seemed to slip sideways as if it were sliding down a ramp towards the ship's port side.

The roar of the one good engine stopped abruptly, and with the cessation of that thunder the silence that followed came like the closing of a door on a noisy classroom. And into this silence fell a cracking sound, as of a branch of a tree snapping off in a gale. A moment later the *Radgate* shuddered as the plane struck her hull. It seemed to strike the water and the ship at the same instant, so that the drag of the water took away some of the force of the impact. Yet it was enough to make the ship lurch and throw Mason's weight against the strap of the Oerlikon.

He recovered his balance, unhooked the strap, and let the gun rest. And as he did so he saw a jet of fire leap into the air on the port side and fall with a fearful hissing sound on the roof of the wheelhouse.

"Holy Jesus!" Gates shouted. "It's petrol."

The impact of the plane against the ship's side had thrown the jet high into the air, a jet lit by the burning engine. Now it was beginning to eat away at the timber, black smoke mingling with the crimson colour of the flame.

Mason ran towards the wheelhouse where he knew a foam extinguisher was kept, but before he could reach the door he heard a man screaming, and it was screaming such as he had never heard or ever wished to hear.

He saw the whole wheelhouse lit up by a torch — and the torch was Scarr. He was aflame from head to foot, a human wick soaked in petrol. Mason saw his hair burning, his face so contorted with agony that it seemed the face of a demon out of hell rather than that of a man. He thrust out his arms as if he were feeling his way, and the arms were firebrands, the flesh on the hands seeming to swell and bubble with the heat.

The cry, inarticulate, terrifying, came pouring out of his throat. He stumbled in the doorway, half fell, and came on. His mouth was open; it was like a ghastly hole in his face from which the screams came searing forth. His eyes stared, without seeing.

Mason yelled: "Stop, Scarr, stop, for God's sake!"

He was wrenching himself out of his duffel coat, intending to wrap Scarr in it in an attempt to stifle the flames. But Scarr did not hear and did not heed the shout. He went stumbling past with the heat flowing from him as from the open door of a furnace. He climbed up on to the rail of the bridge, swayed there for a moment, and then flung himself downward and outward.

In his brain there must have been some idea of casting himself into the water, so that the sea might quench the fire that was consuming him; but he made an error of judgment; instead of clearing the ship's side he fell just short of his target. His head struck the iron of the bulwark and his body, still flaming, but no longer in pain, fell like a meteor to the deck.

7

Return

THE *Radgate* was butting up-channel in the darkness of a June night in a long convoy of little ships. She was empty, unballasted, and jumping about in fairly lively fashion, even though the English Channel was not in one of its bad moods. There was, however, enough swell to impart sufficient motion to the *Radgate* to upset a stomach not hardened to such lifting and falling.

It was a night not of completely impenetrable blackness; some stars were shining, and ahead and astern of the *Radgate* and also on her starboard beam could be discerned the dark, formless shadows that were other ships.

Mason, going on watch at midnight, was struck by the quietness. After the noise of the past three days — the noise of winches, of gunfire, of aircraft engines, of men shouting — this hush that had fallen on the ship seemed unnatural. He had become used to threading his way past the sappers on the foredeck; now they had gone, camped down somewhere on the beaches of Arromanches, working on other ships, working feverishly to get the ammunition and stores unloaded, working always against time to build up a reserve for the armies that must force open the doors of their bridgehead and go fanning out across Europe.

The *Radgate* had carried out her first task; now she was going back to London for reloading. But Scarr was not going with her. He would never go back. He would never again be late on parade, late in returning from leave; for him it was finished. But in Mason's mind he still lived, still with the flames wrapping him, still with that terrible inhuman face, swelling and blistering in the fire, still with the screams coming from the dark cavity of his mouth.

Mason climbed the starboard ladder to the bridge and found Gates leaning on the gun.

"Glad you've come," Gates said.

"My God, I'm tired."

"You're not the only one. Go and get your head down."

Gates went away, and Mason thought about sleep. He wanted some more for himself; his eyes felt sticky, as though they had been painted with glue, as though the eyelids needed some props to keep them up. In the last three days he had had only a few brief snatches of sleep, never more than an hour at a time, perhaps amounting to no more than four hours in all. His body ached, as though the lack of rest had had the same effect as a beating of the limbs. The muscles of his legs and arms were stiff, and he seemed to move in a semi-stupor, like a man in a dream.

He breathed in deeply, trying to keep awake. He turned his whole mind on this problem of keeping awake. It was a task that had been set him. If he were to rest his arms on the edge of the gun-box, if he were to lower his head on to those arms, he would drift off into sleep at once. He must not do that; he had to keep awake — awake.

He began to think of incidents that

had occurred in the past three days — pictures that had imprinted themselves on the sensitive plate of his memory, to remain there, fixed for ever.

A Spitfire gliding out from the land with a hole in its wing and a twisted, motionless propeller, diving suddenly into the sea as if a hand had thrust it down. The first batch of German prisoners coming out on a float, looking drab and sullen and stunned. The ships that were to form the breakwater settling slowly upon the bottom like broody hens settling on clutches of eggs — ships that had come at last to the end of their journeying, to be holed by their own crews so that they might form a shield for others. The massive concrete caissons of Mulberry harbour, floating across the Channel and being manoeuvred into position, just as had been planned so many months before. The D.U.K.W's passing from the water to the land and vanishing into the distance. The flicker of the guns at night, like lightning against the dark background of the sky. An airman's body floating past in its inflated life-jacket, the face staring sightlessly up at the white clouds and the gulls screaming overhead. A German plane sweeping along the beach, and an ammunition dump exploding with a great roar, thrusting up a plume of fire and smoke. Shells dropping like stones into the sea, sending up spurts of water like sudden fountains, dying at once. The masses of Allied aircraft flying overhead. The tiny puppets falling on the sand, running and falling, running and falling . . .

But above all he remembered Scarr — that was the image that would not leave him, Scarr rushing from the wheelhouse and falling to the bulwark and the deck. The petrol that soaked him had continued to burn for a while; it was like a bundle of old rags flaming and smoking in the corner formed by the bulwark and the midships superstructure; there was a smell of burning flesh. Then somebody had brought up a fire-extinguisher, and the body had been covered in foam, as though there had been some idea of washing away the evidence.

It was Mr Gregory who, almost single-handed, had put out the fire on the bridge. With a task to do, he had become no longer nervous, no longer jittery, but a capable ship's officer, marshalling his fire-fighting reserves before the flames could have a chance to spread to the cargo. The plane itself had sunk almost immediately, leaving only a few pools of fire floating on the surface of the water, fire which quickly died.

It had been a near thing for the *Radgate*, a very near thing; but the ship had escaped with no more than a dent or two in her hull, some blistered paint, and a few charred planks. No one but Scarr had had so much as a little finger injured. Scarr had been unlucky — that was all.

Mason heard Captain Garner come out of the wheelhouse on to the wind of the bridge. He could smell Garner's pipe, and when he turned he could see the red glow of the pipebowl like a tiny furnace ignited for the especial purpose of warming Garner's bulbous nose.

"A fine night, sergeant. Hope it stays that way." The voice was harsh and unmusical as ever. "When you come to think of it, sergeant, we're lucky to be doing this trip at all. We're lucky not to be scattered in little bits and pieces somewhere over there." Mason could see the dark outline of his arm sweep away in the direction of France. "A funny thing — Providence. No reason why we should have been spared — not so far as I can see. No reason why that poor young devil should have been taken. But that's how it is." He gave a few puffs at the pipe; the glow in the bowl brightened and died, brightened and died. "Seems to me I was born lucky. Here I've been up and down the East Coast all through the War — planes, mines, subs, E-boats, the whole caboodle — and never a ship sunk under me. Luck; the devil's own luck."

Mason said quietly: "It's not finished yet, sir."

"What's that? Too early to start boasting? You think I'm tempting Providence, ought to be touching wood and crossing my fingers: Is that it?" He laughed, and it was like a series of explosions in the depths of his belly. "I don't worry about that. I'm not superstitious. Maybe the luck will turn; maybe I'll even lose this ship; but it won't be because I boasted of past good fortune. If I'm going to die I'll die, and that's all there is to it. But you don't catch me going about with lucky charms and stepping round ladders and avoiding cross-eyed women and the like. I leave that sort of thing to the mate."

"Mr Gregory? Is he superstitious?"

"I'll say he is. He wouldn't dare go to sea without his rabbit's foot and his abracadabra. If he was to hear you whistling he'd be down on you like a ton of bricks. Lot of mumbo-jumbo, I call it; but it makes him happy. Most sailors are the same. I don't happen to be; that's all."

Mason heard the soft pad of dog's feet on the boards, and saw the two eyes of Cerberus peering at him. Garner stooped and patted the Alsatian's back. "If I needed any charm I'd have you, wouldn't I, boy? You're worth a hundred rabbit's feet."

Garner lapsed into silence, staring into the darkness ahead, trying, perhaps, to gauge the distance between his own ship and the one it was following. Mason, without Garner's voice to keep him awake, found himself nodding off to sleep, his chin dropping on to his chest. He pulled himself up with a jerk, blinking his eyes rapidly in an attempt to clear them of the gumminess which seemed to be holding them shut.

He heard Garner's voice, puzzled: "Now what in hell's that?"

Mason became fully awake. Garner was looking away to starboard, and Mason looked in that direction also. What he saw was a light moving in the sky, coming up from the French coast towards the convoy. It was red, and it was like a bright star moving very rapidly.

"What can that be?" Garner said. "Surely no aircraft would be showing a light."

Mason swung the gun round and brought the sights to bear on this moving star.

"Don't fire unless we're attacked," Garner warned him. "It may be nothing to do with us, and we don't want to advertise our presence."

Mason had had no intention of firing. It was a kind of reflex action, that movement of the gun, something you did under any threat of danger, like a cat unsheathing its claws or a dog baring its teeth.

The light was nearer now, but it was no ordinary light; it was drawn out like the tail of a comet or a flame. A bomber with one of its engines on fire? But it did not sound like a bomber; there was no heavy drone of the bomber's engines; rather it sounded like the stutter of a motor-cycle.

Captain Garner shuffled his feet. "This is a new one on me."

Mason swung the gun up, following the trail of light. It went straight on over the convoy and headed inland. They watched it receding in the distance until they could see it no more, until its sound died away into silence.

"Now tell me, sergeant, what you thought it was," Captain Garner said.

Mason let the gun slip out of his hands, to point straight up at the star-bright sky. "I don't know, sir. I just don't know."

It was some time later when the next light went over — again with that sound as of a popping motor-cycle engine, following the track of the first. It was followed by another, and another.

Garner's pipe made a juicy, sucking noise. He appeared to have been thinking deeply. "What's your opinion on the subject of secret weapons?" he asked. "Our friend Adolf's been yelling about them enough. Do you think he's got one moving at last?"

"A lot of eyewash is what I think," Mason said. "If you really ask me I'd say the secret weapon exists only in Hitler's imagination. It's something he keeps talking about just to bolster up the morale of the German people."

"And yet there might be something in it for all that."

"I'll believe in a secret weapon when I see one. Until then I'll stick to my doubts."

"Just so," Garner said. "But supposing you have already seen one — and heard it to?"

★ ★ ★

Before he came off watch Mason knew he was going to be sick. He had not been sea-sick for nearly two years, but he knew the taste of it — the hot, bitter liquid at the back of the throat, the leaden feeling in the head. He was annoyed that he should feel sick now — there was no reason for it, the Channel was not even rough; there was only this slight see-saw motion of the ship, and he had gone through Atlantic gales without a trace of queasiness. So why should he be afflicted now? Perhaps it was the tiredness; perhaps that had something to do with it. Whatever the reason, he knew that he was going to be sick.

Nevertheless, he held it in until Gates came up to relieve him at the changing of the watch, refusing to give way in the presence of Captain Garner.

"I left you a slice of ham," Gates said. "No bread left, but plenty of biscuits. Everything all right?"

"Everything," Mason said, and went down the ladder before Gates could strike up a conversation. When he got to the deck he let it go, leaning over the bulwark and vomiting into the darkness. At once he felt relieved. Perhaps it had not been sea-sickness at all, but merely the result of something he had eaten. His pride would not allow him to believe that he could be sea-sick with the Channel no rougher than this. Yes, certainly it was something he had eaten.

He went into the tiny cabin in the forecastle and avoided looking at the slice of fat ham that Gates had left for him. He dragged off his duffel coat, kicked off his boots, and slipped out of battle-blouse and trousers. One foot on the lower bunk, a heave, and he was up. The blankets were still warm from Gates's occupation; he wriggled down under them, put his head on the pillow where Gates's head had so lately rested, and, with the sea dashing against the curve of the bows not twelve inches from his ear, he was in a moment fast asleep.

★ ★ ★

The convoy passed through the Strait of Dover early in the morning, a long double line of little ships herded by small craft of the Royal Navy. Between them and the French coast Swordfish aircraft and thundering motor-launches laid a smoke-screen. It was like a bank of fog drifting before the wind. Away on the port side were the Dover cliffs, showing up in the early-morning sunlight like great white teeth. But for the sound of the Swordfish and the launches, it was a peaceful morning; there was no interference from the guns of Calais, no trouble from E-boat or submarine or bomber.

"It's getting so quiet these days," Garner said, "you could almost call it a pleasure cruise. Not that I'm grumbling. It can stay that way as far as I'm concerned."

"You've been through the Strait a good many times, I expect," Mason said. "Did you ever get shelled from the French coast?"

Garner rubbed his chin where the morning bristle was like a worn-down flue-brush. "Shelled — yes; once or twice. But I never knew any ships to be sunk. It gave you a scare, though."

By late afternoon the *Radgate* was anchored again in view of Southend Pier. The following day she moved up-river and worked her way past the lock gates into the calm and dirty water of the East India docks.

A man shouted: "What's it like over there?" But the answer was confused. How was it possible to convey to anyone who had not seen it all the splendour and the tragedy? Here was the *Radgate* with her dented hull, her blistered paint, and her charred woodwork: these tell the story.

"What's it like over there?"

"Not bad."

"You had a bit of excitement by the look of things."

"Yes — a bit."

"Still, you're home again, aren't you?"

"Yes — home again."

They moved into the dock smoothly, easily, fenders groaning in the sandwich between concrete and iron, men shouting orders, working levers, carrying ropes to slip over bollards; it was the same as ever, nothing different, nothing unusual, the ship moving through the lock gates and coming to rest against the quay just as quietly and unfussily as if it had been on no more than a voyage to Newcastle or Hull or Aberdeen, and not on the greatest seaborne invasion that had ever been known. But for the blackened wood and the blistered paint no one would have guessed from looking at the little coaster that she had been engaged in the business of war and not of peace.

And there was no change in the crew; they had seen history being made, had indeed helped to make it, but that did not alter the necessity for carrying out the usual duties concerned with the docking of the ship. Winches had still to be driven, ropes made fast, orders obeyed. Nothing had been altered; they had delivered their cargo and had come back for more; that was all there was to it.

"Did you see the paratroops dropping?"

"Yes, we saw them — poor bastards."

"Did you go ashore?"

"No, we didn't go ashore. What should we go ashore for?"

"Did you see any Germans?"

"Yes — prisoners."

"Were you bombed?"

"No much. A few shells; they didn't hit us."

There was so much to tell — and yet

so little. You could not encompass the grand sweep of it all. The things you remembered were not important: a gull's wing casting a shadow on the face of a dead man floating in the sea; the glint of sunlight on the window of a house; the American commander of a landing-craft chewing on the soggy end of a cigar; the tentative way a tank felt its way down the ramp, touched the sand, and then went plunging forward; the ear-blasting slam of a 14-inch gun; a balloon, ripped by shell-splinters, falling like a dead bird; parachutes dropping like thistledown; the white bursts of anti-aircraft shells like stuttering punctuation on the blue page of the sky; a sailor trying to disentangle a length of rope from the propeller of a launch; the dull, dead look of 5.5 inch shells as they came up out of the hold; the smell of oil, rank and heavy, and the beautiful colours of an oil-patch on the water; the sound of a man singing . . .

"It must have been worth seeing."

"Yes — it was worth seeing."

* * *

Mason went aft to inspect the twin Oerlikon. Sims and Vickers were giving it a final pull-through, and Mason examined each barrel in turn.

"All right. They'll do. You've got all your magazines seen to?"

"Yes, sergeant." Sims spoke with a trace of severity, and Mason detected the note in the gunlayer's voice. He ought to have known better than to ask the question; he knew that he could rely on the conscientious Sims.

"How many rounds did you fire?"

"Ninety-six." Sims pointed to a sandbag. "Empty cases. I suppose they'll be collected?"

"If anybody thinks about it. Most likely we'll have them left on our hands, just getting in the way. If we chucked them overboard somebody would soon want to know where they were. That's how it is."

Vickers said: "You know those things we saw flying over as we came up the Channel? Looks like they were flying-bombs or pilotless aircraft or something."

"Where'd you get that idea?" Mason asked.

"It's in the paper. One of the dockers gave us one."

Captain Garner waylaid Mason as he went back to the chart-room. "How about secret weapons now? Do you still say it's eyewash? Flying-bombs, hey! There's nice things for you."

"If that's all he's got up his sleeve," Mason said, "he's in a pretty bad way. It'll take more than a handful of those things to wipe London out."

"Yes, but suppose it isn't just a handful. Suppose he sends five thousand. They'd make a mess; they make one hell of a mess."

He sucked at his pipe, and the tobacco crackled in the bowl like dry twigs. He was in his informal dress — blue dungaree trousers, a leather belt, and a khaki shirt open at the neck. The shirt was in fact open almost to the waist, revealing a V-shaped portion of chest and stomach as hairy as that of an ape. There was something brigandish, piratical, about Captain Garner. With a cutlass slipped into his belt, and a spotted handkerchief about his head, he could have stepped straight into the caste of a buccaneering film set in the Caribbean Sea. Perhaps some distant ancestor had swung from the gibbets of Portsmouth harbour or had retired to a life of ease on his ill-gotten wealth in doomed Port Royal. It might well have been so.

He said, his quick, intelligent eyes peering at Mason through the tobacco smoke: "We'll likely be in port for a few days. I've no doubt your men will be wanting passes. You'd better come along to my cabin and I'll make them out. Might as well make the most of your time."

"Thank you, sir."

"By the way, that kid who was killed — what was his name?"

"Scarr."

"That's it — Scarr. Didn't he have a wife somewhere in London?"

"Dagenham."

"Oh, out there, was it? Do doubt she'll have heard the news officially by now. They're pretty quick off the mark. I don't know whether you're thinking of taking a trip that way. Not much you can do, of course . . . "

"I had thought of it," Mason said. "I

think it would be best if I went there first — get it over. It's not a job I'm particularly keen on."

"It's not a nice job." Garner looked away across the dock to where a steamer of about twice the tonnage of the *Radgate* was being eased into its berth. He was silent for a time, giving that critical operation his whole attention, as though he felt that it could not be successfully accomplished unless he did so. Then, when the steamer was safely linked to the quay, he turned again to Mason. "No, it's not a nice job. Damned if it is."

★ ★ ★

Mason had some difficulty in finding Scarr's house. He seemed to be unfortunate in selecting a succession of half-wits to direct him to the address. Some of them seemed never to have heard the name of the road, staring at him in bewilderment, as if he had asked to be directed to the next world. One man did his best to convince Mason that he had got the address wrong, that he must have done, because there was no such place as that which he was trying to reach. Mason himself had almost come to the same conclusion before, after many false scents, he did at last find himself in the road he was looking for.

It was no more than a link between two more important thoroughfares, a road that appeared to have been laid out for the express purpose of accommodating on either side a row of identical houses — little boxes, so narrow, so tightly packed, that one might have supposed they had been crushed together by placing a bulldozer at each end of the row and exerting pressure. It was as though the houses might once have been squat and fat, but had been made thinner and taller in order to save space.

Mason counted the numbers until he arrived at the one in which Scarr had lived. It was no different from the others; the paint was just as old, just as dull and grimy; it seemed not so much a place to live in as to get away from. Mason, whose home had always been a rambling farmhouse of mellowed stone, with a view of fields and woodland from the windows, wondered how anyone could endure living in these wretched, closed-in hutches.

Now that he had found the house he felt a strong reluctance to go farther. He felt as though he were prying into the secrets of the dead man. This had been Scarr's home, perhaps the one place where he could truly be himself, free from the influence of Army life. Here it was where he had been able to cast off his uniform and become again the civilian. Thinking of this, Mason forgot that he had never liked the man. Scarr was dead now, and all that was past. He might not have been a good soldier — how many were good soldiers? — but in this house he had been more than a soldier; he had been a husband.

It was getting late in the evening now. An Army lorry went past, and Mason wondered what business an Army lorry could have in that road. It seemed to have no military connections; it did not appear to lead anywhere. Two girls waved their hands to the driver of the lorry and giggled. Mason walked up to the front door of the house and pressed the bell-push. He could hear the bell chattering fussily on the other side of the door, and it reminded him of the alarm-bell that had been fixed just above his bunk in the ship in which he had sailed to Russia. It had the same kind of rattle, not really a bell-like sound at all; a woodpecker getting to work on a tin can would have made a similar noise.

The door had apparently been bolted top and bottom, for Mason could hear the bolts being slipped back. A key turned in the lock, and the door opened for the distance of about a foot.

"Mrs Scarr?"

The woman was only partially revealed in the gap, but the amount that was visible gave promise of a great deal more hidden behind the door. It was like the part of an iceberg above the surface which represents only a fraction of the whole. Her face was heavy, flesh-laden, the eyes hostile, the hair flecked with grey. She looked about fifty.

Mason had been expecting some one smaller, younger, more like Scarr himself. But, of course, it was not unknown for a man to marry a woman older and bigger than himself.

"What do you want?" the woman asked.

"It's about Reggie." He had never used that name before, never looked upon Scarr as anything but Gunner Scarr. The 'Reggie' came awkwardly to his tongue.

"What about him?" The woman's mouth opened to let the words through, then closed like the lid of a deed-box. Mason could imagine the mental turning of a key in the lock, preventing any unauthorized words from slipping out.

"I was with him when . . . He was in my detachment . . . I thought . . . "

The woman pulled the door open wider, revealing the submerged four-fifths.

"I suppose you'd better come in." She said it ungraciously, with some reluctance, as though she were letting death into the house.

Mason went in, and she closed the door behind him. It seemed to shut out all the light and all the air. It was as though he were wedged in a dark cupboard with this immense mountain of a woman. Then she had opened another door and was pushing him into what was obviously the best room, used only on special occasions. It was small, and it was crammed full of hideous furniture. It had a dead, stale, fusty smell, as though neither the door nor the heavily curtained window had been opened for months, even years.

"Sit down," the woman said. It was an order rather than an invitation. Mason sat on an uncomfortable leatherette-upholstered chair. He would have liked a cigarette, but in this prim, dustless room it would have seemed sacrilegious to smoke. He looked at the woman, with her heavy features and her grim, straight mouth and accusing eyes, and could have laughed at himself for the picture he had had in his mind of a tearful little widow, sobbing her heart out for the husband she had so lately lost. Well, it was easier this way.

He looked at the furniture, all so neat, so prim, so old-fashioned and so comfortless, and tried to picture Scarr in those surroundings. But it was no use; he did not fit. Perhaps his own slovenliness had been a reaction against this order. Scarr — even now it was hard to realize that he was dead. And by so narrow a margin. Five minutes later, five minutes more spent in this house, and he would have missed his ship; might have missed the invasion; might still have been alive.

The woman shifted on her chair, and Mason saw that she was becoming impatient.

He said: "Mrs Scarr — I — "

"I'm not Mrs Scarr. I'm Mrs Durrant. Reggie was my son-in-law."

"Oh!" He stared at her stupidly. He had been expecting only Mrs Scarr; he had not thought of anyone else being in the house. But, of course, it was only natural that at a time of bereavement like this her mother should come to her.

Mrs Durrant said: "You'll be Sergeant Mason. I've heard about you." She did not say what she had heard, but her manner seemed to imply that it was nothing creditable. Her whole attitude was accusatory. In Mason she seemed to be looking at the representative of those evil forces that had stolen away her son-in-law. Mason was representative of the whole system.

He said awkwardly: "Perhaps I could see Mrs Scarr. Is she in?"

Mrs Durrant folded her arms like two joints of raw, red meat. She was wearing a thin cotton dress; it was a faded yellow, and it bulged in all the wrong places.

"She's in all right. But you can't see her. No; that's quite impossible."

"Oh!" Mason said, and there was a gap in this strained and useless conversation. The silence seemed to hang upon the room like a weight. Mason was hypnotized by the rise and fall of Mrs Durrant's bosom as she breathed; each time she breathed in it seemed that now at last the yellow dress must surely burst its seams; each time her breath came out it was like a sigh of relief that once again the fabric had held firm.

The silence was finally broken by a slight noise from the room above. Mrs Durrant got up at once and went to the door. Half in and half out of the room, with her hand resting on the door-knob, she called: "Is that you, Ella? Did you want anything?"

A woman's voice answered something that Mason failed to catch; and then he heard quite distinctly the sound of a baby crying. It was not until that moment that he remembered that Mrs Scarr had been expecting.

8

The Power to Hurt

IT was late in the evening when Mason left Scarr's house. It had taken him some considerable time to escape from Mrs Durrant, for that majestic woman, once having started to talk, seemed unwilling to leave off. Mason, now impatient to get away, was forced to listen to Mrs Durrant's views on the iniquity of war.

"I lost my own 'usband in the first, so I know what I'm talking about. Durrant was a fine man — you should have seen him. There he is."

Mason, startled by this sudden statement, half expected to see the ghost of the late Mr Durrant walking into the room. But it was a photograph in a gilt frame at which Mrs Durrant was pointing. Mason saw a round, singularly vacant-looking face with protuberant eyes and a waxed moustache.

223

"Sergeant-major, 'e was — 'Orse Artillery. There wasn't much 'e didn't know. Strong, too. Why, 'e could lift me off me feet with one 'and."

Mason would have like to have seen this feat performed. The sergeant-major must have been a Samson. But perhaps in the course of thirty years of widowhood Mrs Durrant had put on a deal of weight.

"With one 'and — just like 'e was lifting a feather. You wouldn't believe."

The deed-box was unlocked now, and the words came out without impediment. Mrs Durrant drew her chair close to the one on which Mason was sitting and held him with a stare that the Ancient Mariner might have envied. She spoke of war, of widowhood, of the miserable size of pensions, of the iniquity of taking husbands into the fighting services at all.

"Single men; they're the ones as should go and fight. They've no responsibilities. They don't 'ave families to support nor nothing like that . . . "

Mason fidgeted on his chair, half rose, and said: "Yes, yes; I see what you mean — " Mrs Durrant put out a hand and pushed him back again. Here he was, the representative of everything about which she desired to complain, and he would have to stay until her complaints were finished.

"You're not married, I suppose?"

"No, as a matter of fact I'm not. But — "

"There you are then. Doesn't it show?"

Mason did not ask what it showed; he was wary of encouraging the flow. If Mrs Scarr had not called again from the room above he doubted whether he would ever have got away. He took advantage of the momentary absence of Mrs Durrant to make his escape.

He wanted to go to Jo at once, but he had to go back to the ship first. On board the *Radgate* he found revelry in progress. He heard the violin first, and then the sound of a man singing in a thin, reedy, high-pitched voice that bore no little resemblance to a squeaking hinge. It was growing dusk now, and it was not until Mason had skirted a silent shadowy crane and climbed up the builder's ladder that served the *Radgate* in place of a gang-plank that the scene was revealed to him in all its splendid, outrageous quality.

On the tarpaulin-covered forward hatch were four men — Captain Garner, the mate Gregory, Chief Engineer Mawby, and the cook. Captain Garner, with a coloured sash knotted about his waist in the manner of a gipsy fiddler, was playing with many false notes a tune that could just be recognized as *The Last Rose of Summer*, while the cook, his eyes turned heavenward, and his arms raised like a man about to catch a Rugby football, was moaning out some dismal song that seemed to have no connexion whatever with the fiddle's tune.

As complement to this musical performance, the mate and the engineer, their natural antipathy apparently swept away, were dancing with linked arms a peculiar species of hornpipe, their trousers rolled above the knee, their podgy legs glimmering palely in the gloom, and their shoes thundering like horses' hooves on the hatch-cover. Sole spectator of this revel — and one who obviously disapproved of the whole affair — was

Cerberus. He was walking round and round the hatch with his tail between his legs, and every now and then he would look up at his master as though doubtful of that man's continuing sanity, whine briefly, and then walk on.

Mason jumped down from the bulwark and stood at the head of the ladder, watching silently. A little cluster of bottles and glasses at one corner of the hatch was visual evidence of the cause of this dancing and singing, this breaking down of the normal barriers of dislike. Only the dog was sober.

Garner suddenly noticed Mason. He gave a final flourish with his bow and then stood, swaying slightly like a particularly stout flower exposed to the wind, with the bow in one hand and the violin in the other.

"Who's that coming 'board my ship? Have you p'mission, sir? Have you warrants, sealed and signed by highest authority?" Without warning he raised his voice to a yell that seemed to split the air like the crack of a twelve-pounder gun. "Ho there! Stand by to repel boarders!"

The mate and the engineer, losing

their grip on each other and at the same time their grip on equilibrium, fell to the canvas and lay there panting and gasping like a couple of monster fish just hauled from the sea.

Captain Garner, focusing his eyes on Mason, suddenly recognized him as one who had a perfect right to board the ship. "So it's you, sergeant. Give the sergeant a drink. Give him a drink, blast you!"

The cook, as though completely unconscious of the fact that both the fiddling and the dancing had come to a stop, was still singing away undeterred. Captain Garner turned on him savagely, as if the sound had just penetrated to this senses.

"Stow that bloody noise. You sound like a ruptured siren. What's up with you? Have you got a belly-ache or something?"

The cook broke off in the middle of a top note and looked pained. "Do you object to my voice, sir?"

"Voice, d'you call it? Voice! Sounds more like a damn cow with foot-and-mouth disease and half an udder. Voice, he says! A rat howling in a sewer would make a better job of it."

The cook said, with a dignity which hardly matched his appearance: "I'd have you know, sir, that I studied singing in Milan under Gordini."

"Studied underneath the arches. Milan, Gordini! Get away with you!"

"I got proof. I can show you. I got certificates."

"Damned bits of paper prove nothing. Give the sergeant a drink, can't you? Stificates! Bloody forgeries — all of 'em. Stificates, with a voice like that!"

The cook began to weep. "My voice has been much admired. In the best circles too — the very best circles." His legs suddenly crumpled under him and he sat down hard on the tarpaulin. Cerberus came and sniffed at him and went way. "Even the dogs despise me now," he said. "What is there left in life? I'd be better dead."

As if in a fit of absent-mindedness, he stretched his hands towards the bottles, filled a glass with gin, and swallowed it in one draught. "Poison," he said. "Filthy poison. Mother's ruin."

"The trouble with you," Garner said,

planting his feet wide and pointing unsteadily at the cook with his bow, "the trouble with you is you're drunk — drunk as a newt. You aren't fit to be on board a decent, God-fearing ship. If it wasn't for this violin in my hand — which I don't wish to damage — I'd throw you overside."

The cook poured himself another glass of gin. "I've served in the best families. I've cooked for crowned heads."

"Crowned arses."

"Do not insult me, sir! I am a man of breeding."

"Something must have gone wrong," Garner said.

The cook looked sadly at his glass with his one good eye, his lank black hair falling over his forehead. "You see fit to torment me, sir. Very well. You are the captain and are king on board this vessel. I bow to your authority." He did in fact bow his head as far as the glass, which, coming into contact with his lips, seemed naturally to tip itself up.

"That bloody cook's drinking more than his fair share," Mr Gregory stated. "Ain't that so?"

He looked at Mawby for corroboration, but the engineer was staring as though fascinated at his own white legs. He kept taking the flesh between his finger and thumb and pressing it, apparently in order to discover whether it were real.

"I have connexions in the Government," the cook said. "There are things I could tell you, but" — he put a long forefinger against the side of his nose — "I am sworn to secrecy." He took another sup of gin, and the glass eye stared unwaveringly straight ahead, a model of rectitude, while the other moved from side to side. "Garibaldi," he said with sudden fierceness. "Garibaldi was a damned villain. I always said he'd come to a bad end. Now look."

"Look at what?" Garner asked, growing confused.

"At the mess we're in — all of us — every mother's son — every whore's bastard — "

"You mind your bloody language," Garner said severely. "This is a respectable ship."

The cook gave a short, mirthless laugh, like the sudden bark of a startled dog, and drank some more gin.

"When I was a boy — " Gregory began.

"You a boy," Garner scoffed. "Don't give us that bilge. You never were a boy. You were born old."

"On the contrary — a very nice, modest, well-behaved little boy. I was in the choir."

"I knew you had secrets."

Mawby seemed to lose interest in his own white legs. He began to roll his trousers down. "My grandma was a great lover of poetry," he said. "She could recite the whole of *Paradise Lost*."

"You damned liar," Garner said without rancour. "That's the worst of ships like this — you get so many liars on board." He noted Mason again. "Why in hell doesn't somebody give the sergeant a drink? Here — come and get one for yourself. Dont stand there like a dummy; you make me nervous. Help yourself, can't you?"

Mason walked across to the little store of liquor at the corner of the hatch-cover. There were three bottles of rum, two of gin, and one of whisky. Each of them had been partly emptied, revealing a lack of system in the drinking. There were only four glasses, all of which had been used. Mason had been too long in the Army to be squeamish. He took a glass and poured himself a tot from one of the rum-bottles. He tipped it down his throat, and the raw spirit seemed to burn a pathway down into his stomach, where it began to stir up trouble with the gastric juices.

"What do you think of it?" Garner asked.

Mason jerked a thumb at the cook, who had now stretched himself out at full length on the hatch as though preparing for sleep. "At a rough guess I'd say it was something that he concocted in the galley."

"I resent that," the cook said. "Let me tell you that I have distilled the finest illixers you could imagine. I have been distiller-in-chief to the Sultan of — " A snore concluded the sentence. The cook had fallen asleep.

"That man," Garner said, "is drunk. Strictly speaking, he isn't fit to prepare food for swine. One of these days he'll poison the lot of us." He tucked the violin under his chin again and plucked at a string as if with some intention of playing pizzicato. The string broke under this heavy treatment, curled up, and lashed him in the eye. He swore, dropped the violin, and kicked it across the hatch, flinging the bow after it.

"If music be the food of love," Mawby said, delving up some memory of poetry imparted by his long-dead grandmother, "play on."

Garner looked at him sourly. "If you want any more music you can make it yourself. What you think I am — a one-man band?"

"There's no such thing," Gregory said. "How could one man play a whole band? Now, I ask you."

Garner eyed him spitefully. A certain lack of friendliness seemed to be developing in the party. "You don't get me on that lark. You know as much about one-man bands as I do. I know the game — you say you don't believe there is such a thing, and then you get me demonstrating and before I know where I am I'm moving my arms and legs like a monkey on a string. But you don't get me doing that."

"All right," Gregory said, "if that's the way you feel. But I still don't believe there is such a thing as a one-man band."

"You're an ignorant bastard. Everybody's seen them."

"Not me. I never saw one in my life. How do they work the instruments?"

"They have some strapped to their elbows and some fixed on their shoulders. They use their feet too."

The mate was sitting cross-legged on the hatch-cover, his face registering nothing but innocent, childlike interest.

"But how do they work them? That's what I want to know. You don't mean to tell me a man can play a banjo with his toes."

"I'll give you banjo," the captain said belligerently. "You shut your face before I put my fist in it. Where's that sergeant? Damned if it isn't getting too dark to see to drink. Hey, sergeant; what — " He broke off suddenly to stare up into the sky, beyond the shadowy outline of the masts and rigging, and the tall, giraffe-like shapes of the cranes, up to where the stars were beginning to appear like touches of gilt paint on a church roof. "There's another of them — another of those blasted doodle-bugs."

It flared across the spires of masts and cranes, its engine sounding louder than any that Mason had previously heard, perhaps because it was so much closer. They stared up at it, that flame in the sky, waiting for the engine to cut out, waiting for that brief silence when the bomb would be falling, and then the blast of the explosion. The coming of the bomb seemed to have sobered them all. They listened until it had passed over. Then Garner said: "To hell with this. I'm turning in."

He walked away, a little unsteady on his feet, with the dog following him. The mate and the engineer went away too. They left the cook asleep on the hatch with the bottles and the glasses and Garner's misused violin, with the wide sky above and the empty hold below. Mason thought about waking him, but decided not to. He shrugged his

shoulders and climbed up to the chart-
room.

As always, the street door was open, but
the house was quiet — dark and quiet
as some abandoned temple. Inside the
air was close, with that peculiar odour
of rottenness and decay that seemed to
belong to this building as by right.

Mason had brought a small pocket
torch from the ship, and, following the
thin white finger of its beam, he climbed
the bare wooden stairs, treading softly to
avoid waking any of the people asleep
behind their closed door. Little more
than a week had passed since he had
last been here, yet in that time so much
had happened that it seemed almost like
a miracle to find the house unchanged.
To Mason the smell of the place, telling
him more than anything else that this
was indeed where he wanted to be, had
come with a sense of relief. The house
was here; it did exist. Jo, then, must
exist also, though there had been times
when he had doubted whether she and

the house were anything more than the memories of a dream. But now he knew that the house was real, and that Jo must be real also.

But then again that feeling of the immensity of time separating the present from the day when he had left her returned to plague him, and he experienced an agony of fear that she might have gone away, packed her few possessions, left the lodging, and vanished out of his life for ever. The thought spurred him on to a final rush up the last few stairs and along the corridor to the door of her room.

He did not knock, but for a moment he stood with his hand on the knob, breathing rapidly. He switched off the torch and dropped it into his pocket, and as he stood there, breathing deeply in that brief pause of expectation and doubt, the house seemed to be breathing also, breathing like some monster settled in a long, deep sleep from which it would have been foolhardy to have awakened it. Then he turned the handle and pushed the door.

It resisted, but only slightly. He could hear something sliding along the floor, and he knew what it was — a box in which Jo kept a jumble of odds and ends — shoe-brushes, dusters, an electric iron, worn-out stockings. She had told him that this was what she put against the door because of the broken lock, and he had scoffed at the idea of trusting a box of junk to keep intruders out. 'I know it's no good,' she had said, 'But it's something. Anyway, I'm not scared. I told you.'

Yes, she had told him. But he had been scared for her. 'I don't like it. Anyone might come in. You ought to get it seen to.' And now he had been away all this age of time and still she had not had it seen to; the lock was still broken; she was still protected by nothing better than a box of junk. He did not push the door far — only far enough to open a gap through which he could squeeze his body. Then he slipped into the room and closed the door softly behind him.

He did not switch on the light, because he could see the square of the window where the black-out board had been taken down to let some air into the room. The objects that he remembered were there like shadows — the cheap, flimsy wardrobe, the chairs, the chest of drawers, the bed. He walked softly across to the bed and stood looking down at the dim outline of her head on the pillow. He could hear the light sound of her breathing. She slept like a child, untroubled, with her short hair like shading on the margins of her head.

Mason felt a surge of love for her that made him tremble. He knelt down by the bed and kissed her on the cheek, very gently, as though he were afraid to waken her, afraid that she might no longer want him. He had been away.

The thinness of her face was not apparent in the semi-darkness; there was no definition about it; there was just the vague outline and the shading of hair. The cheek felt cool to Mason's lips, smooth and soft and cool. He kissed her so lightly that she did not waken, did not even stir, her breath coming and going unhurried, as though her mind were completely at peace, as though fear, pain, sadness — none of these could touch her; nor the sleep-destroying

240

gnawings of ambition.

A movement of air from the window touched the back of Mason's neck like a cool finger stirring the hair. He had become calm. He wanted to savour this moment endlessly, this oasis in time, this pause before Jo should awaken. He had been afraid — afraid that she might not be here, afraid that he might not be able to return to her, afraid that he might never see her again. But now there was no more fear; he had found her. Even the gap of days that in his mind had lengthened out into weeks and months and years, even that gap had not taken her from him. She was here, close to him; so close that he could hear her breathing; so close that he had been able to touch her cheek with his lips. The peace that had come upon him was so sweet that he hesitated to break the spell. He felt that he would gladly have spent the rest of his life watching beside her thus, asking nothing more.

She awoke as silently as she had slept. There was no sense of shock to find him there beside her bed, no exclamation of fear. It was as though he had been

241

present to her in a dream, and now, waking, she found that it was more than a dream, that he was there in fact.

He had his back to the dim suggestion of light that came from the window, so that she could not have recognized him; to her he was no more than a dark shadow crouching there; but she knew that it was he; there was no hint of doubt in her voice. It was as though she accepted his presence as something completely natural — as she had accepted his going, so she accepted his return — now — in the night — any time. It did not matter when he came; she would be there to welcome him back.

"Peter!"

That was her voice — the voice with its slight metallic timbre that he had tried to recapture in memory without succeeding. Now he heard it again, and wondered why it would not come to him in imagination. Perhaps it was too subtle a thing to be recalled in absence; perhaps the intonation had to be heard, and having been heard would not remain in the memory, but like a bubble trapped in the hand was gone immediately, vanished into the air.

"So you've come at last."

"At last! Has it seemed long to you too?"

"As long as years. Ages. Kiss Me."

She was sitting up in the bed, lifting her face to his. He put his arms about her thin shoulders, and could feel the bones under the skin. He kissed her, and then laughed.

"You haven't got fat while I've been away — long as it's been."

"No," she said. "But I'm pretty, aren't I? It's dark enough. In this light I could pass for pretty whoever was looking at me. Don't you think so?"

"To me you're more than pretty. You're beautiful."

"Ah, you're laughing at me again."

"No, Jo; not now."

"You mean it? Really? Oh, I wanted you to come. I wanted to hear you say these things again — all these nice things. It doesn't matter whether they're true or not. Sometimes you make me believe you mean them."

"I do mean them."

"Do you love me, then?"

"I love you, Jo."

He kissed her again, glad that he had come, glad that he had not waited until the next day.

"What kept you so long away?" she asked. "Why didn't you come back before?"

"I couldn't. It wasn't possible. And it's only been a week — not much more."

"Only a week. I don't believe it. And where have you been all that week? No, no; don't tell me. I don't want to know. I don't want to know anything. I just want you here. That's all that matters. When you went away I thought I wouldn't care. If you were gone and never came back I wasn't going to let it trouble me. I didn't mean to let anything like that trouble me — ever. I was independent, see? Not going to let any man make a fool of me. Do you understand what I'm talking about?"

"I don't have to understand. Just go on talking."

"I was the clever girl — the one who wasn't ever going to get herself hurt. And what happens? Why, you come along.

244

Make it all nonsense."

"Have I hurt you?"

"I don't know. Perhaps not yet — not much. But you will. You've made me so I can be hurt, don't you see?"

"I'll never hurt you, Jo — never."

"Cross your heart?"

"Cross my heart."

She laughed suddenly, happily, and brushed the hair back from her forehead with one sweep of the hand. "Aren't we a pair of fools, talking about getting hurt or not getting hurt. What does it matter? If it comes it comes. This is all that really matters — this now — while you're here with me. I won't think of anything else, anything after. I don't have to, do I?"

"You don't have to do anything you don't want to do."

"And you? Don't you have to either?"

"Yes. I have to go away."

"And you'd rather stay here? Stay here and tell me how pretty I am. Perhaps it's true. Perhaps I never looked in the right glass. Now just how pretty am I? As pretty as — "

"Venus?"

"Yes — Venus. Am I that pretty?"

"Prettier. She was too fat."

"Well, I'm not fat." She held up one of her arms. "Look. Nobody could say I was, could they?"

"You're a skinny child, and I love you," Mason said, laughing.

"I'm not a child."

"No, Jo, you're not a child. And I still love you."

He kissed her again, and heard the sound of the rat gnawing in the wall.

9

Doodle-bugs

IN the morning the dockers came and opened up the *Radgate*'s holds, and a crane moved along its rails like some madman's design for a railway truck, rolling with ponderous inevitability along the lines until it came into position. Then it swivelled to the right and to the left, as though testing the flexibility of its great iron skeleton, and, finding this in order, prepared for the day's work.

A motor-trolley nosed its way out of a transit shed with a load of packing-cases, seemed to hesitate for a moment like a traveller uncertain of his way, then rolled towards the *Radgate*. It was the first drop in the river of cargo flowing towards her holds.

Mason arrived on board in time for breakfast and found the cook suffering from a hangover and in a very sour mood. He had prepared some gruesome-looking mess that might have been the mashed-up remains of countless previous meals. He slapped a helping on to Mason's plate from an iron spoon, and the blob spread itself slowly out like a pile of flour with the weevil in it.

"What's this?" Mason asked.

The cook had not shaved. He had probably not washed either. He was smoking a very badly rolled cigarette from which the ash hung in a long, drooping finger, threatening at any moment to project itself into the food. His good eye stared at Mason venomously while the other remained aloof, apparently gazing at some point two feet above his head.

"If you don't like it, you know what you can do."

Mason did not pursue the question any further. In his present mood one could expect nothing but rudeness from the cook. He seemed to have forgotten the manners that must have been his when working for the best families.

"You're damned lucky to get anything, I'm telling you."

It was not, in fact, destined to be a good day for him: a fireman, also

248

suffering from the after-effects of an evening ashore, took one look at the mess on his plate and slammed it back in the cook's face, crushing two inches of burning cigarette into his mouth. The victim retaliated vigorously with a pan of hot grease, and for a short while the galley was a battlefield.

Gates, who witnessed the contest, was highly amused. He confided to Mason that what he really wanted to see was one of the antagonists thrown into the dock. "You don't get such a lot of fun these days. Does you good to see a bit of an argument. Livens things up."

The bit of an argument ended with the cook and the fireman both exhausted, one the possessor of a cut lip and a bleeding nose, the other of a black eye and a brand-new gap in the range of his front teeth. It was some time before the cooking returned to an even keel.

Altogether an air of gloom seemed to have settled on the ship — a gloom all the deeper by contrast with the effervescent feelings as the vessel docked on the previous day. Then everyone had been filled with the sense of a task completed, of a danger passed safely through. They had been in a mood for celebration; and they had celebrated — perhaps too well. Now the sad, stale aftermath of that celebration was depressing their spirits, making them snappish and short-tempered.

Mr Gregory and Mr Mawby, those two brotherly hornpipers of the previous evening, encountering each other on deck, had taken one look, snarled something highly insulting, and had then gone their separate ways. Mr Mawby was reported later to be sitting on a box in the engine-room, staring fixedly and gloomily at a boiler as though expecting it at any moment to burst and end his worldly cares for ever, and Mr Gregory could be observed wandering about the deck like a very corpulent wolf, searching with bloodshot eyes for all the sins that dockers are habitually addicted to while loading a ship.

Captain Garner, meanwhile, was in a similar smouldering fury. Seated in his cabin, he was attempting with the aid of glue and plywood, screws and bits of wire, to repair the damage that rough treatment and a night on the open deck had caused to his violin. A seaman having the temerity to thrust his head into the cabin and question Garner concerning some trivial matter had retreated hastily under a hail of abuse and the threat of having the dog turned on him.

Taken as a whole, there seemed to be a certain lack of the milk of human kindness on board the *Radgate*, with every one keeping himself very much to himself and resenting any intrusion on his private miseries. Whether the dockers, who had fallen on the ship like an invading army, noticed this atmosphere of depression and antagonism Mason could not say. He had never looked on dockers as particularly sensitive men, and he supposed it was all one to them if the cook was at loggerheads with the fireman or the mate with the chief engineer. Their job was simply to fill the ship with another cargo of high explosive, and this they set about doing in their own way and at their own pace, which was, so Mason observed, a good deal less hectic than that of the soldiers who had unloaded her on the other side of the English Channel.

But perhaps the sappers had had more incentive to work rapidly when they could hear the rumbling of the guns, and knew that other soldiers might die for lack of those shells which they were dragging from the ship's hold. The dockers had no such spur; they loaded this cargo no faster than a thousand others; it was no different from any other, except in that particular quality of explosiveness which made it a little more dangerous to handle, and made safety precautions rather more necessary. The mate, detecting a man smoking in the after hold, had to be restrained from going at him with a marline-spike. "Does he want us all blown sky-high? If I had my way I'd make him eat his cigarettes — packet and all." Mr Gregory's head was still very sore.

Once or twice the sound of a flying-bomb was heard, and the dockers seemed to become restive. Mason heard some of them talking about the damage in different parts of London. No one had actually seen the effect of a bomb, but they had all heard that it was something quite colossal. "More than a block-buster, mate. One o' them things'll blow a whole row of houses down — straight it will."

"It's the blast, y'see. Don't make much of a hole, but the blast does it."

The man who had made the last remark had his back to Mason, but there was something about the voice and something about the shape of the man's head that reminded him of Dave. It was an unpleasant reminder, like the scar on his hand. He wanted to forget Dave — to forget that he had called Jo 'kid.'

"If one o' them doodle-bugs landed anywhere near this ship it'd be curtains for the lot of us," the docker said. He rubbed his hands on his trousers, as though the sweat of fear was making the palms damp. "Why don't somebody do something about it? Are they just going to wait until all London's knocked to bits?" He turned his head and looked at Mason as though accusing him of letting the flying-bombs shatter London. Mason saw that it was not Dave; this man was older, and his face had a pinched look, the look of a man with a permanent grievance, a grudge against authority.

"What would you suggest?" Mason asked.

"Me? I wouldn't suggest nothing. Ain't my job, see? I know my job and I do it. Bombs and suchlike is the department of them what wears the King's uniform. Am I right or am I wrong?"

"You'd better write a letter to Churchill," Mason said.

Midway through the morning a sergeant of the Maritime Artillery arrived with the gunner who was to replace Scarr — a fair-haired, intelligent-looking youngster whose name was Braddock. Braddock was not yet twenty; he had been in the Army less than a year, and Mason realized with something of a shock that this smooth-faced boy had probably been still at school at the time of Dunkirk. The War had been going on a long time — too long.

"Braddock, eh? What regiment?"

"The Third, sergeant."

"Oh — North Shields. It's a while since I was there."

Quite a while, but he remembered

Shields. He had been up there for his gunlayer's course. He remembered the daily crossing of the Tyne to the south side where H.M.S *Satellite* lay. He had had a good time of it, and had left with some regret.

"How long since you were there?"

"About three weeks, sergeant."

"The Y.M. still functioning?"

"Oh, yes."

"All right, Braddock. Rickman will show you where to stow your kit. You'll have to take a bunk in the crew's fo'c'sle, I'm afraid. D'you mind?"

"No, I don't mind."

"All the same if he did," the embarkation sergeant said, "Beggars can't be chooser."

"Are we beggars?"

"Might as well be." The sergeant was a soft-looking man with a nervous tic in the left side of his face and bitten-down fingernails. He shot a glance at Mason as though weighing him up. "Nasty business, that — Scarr, I mean. You saw it, I suppose?"

"Well, naturally. You don't suppose I was asleep?"

"No, no, of course not. Hardly likely."

He laughed, unsure of himself, unsure of Mason. "Was it bad? I mean, did he suffer much, do you think?"

"Try being burned alive some time and see how it feels." Mason was not impressed by this sergeant. How did these fellows get their shore jobs, he wondered. This man looked as nervous as a new boy at school. But perhaps there were reasons why he was like that; he might not always have been so. Perhaps that was why he was ashore — because he was not fit to go to sea.

"I've brought you some mail. Gates — that's one of your men, isn't it?"

"Gates and Rickman — they're the two."

He sorted through the letters, found two for Gates, one for Rickman, and one for Mason. Mason knew at once by the handwriting that it was from Clare — and he had not yet answered her previous letter.

"Well," the sergeant said, "I shall have to go. Got some more ships to visit. Anything you want me to do for you?"

"Nothing, thanks."

"Right, then; I'll be off."

Mason took Gates and Rickman their letters, then went with his own to the chart-room, which happened fortunately to be unoccupied — even Cerberus being absent from his favourite resting-place on the settee. Mason used his clasp-knife to slit open the envelope. He drew out the folded sheets, and a small rectangle of card fell to the floor. He picked it up and saw that it was a photograph of Clare — a rather amateur snapshot taken, he could see, on the tennis lawn in front of the Hordern's farmhouse. The house with its walls overgrown with Virginia creeper and its diamond-paned windows formed a background to the picture of the girl who would one day inherit it.

Mason lit a cigarette and relaxed on the settee, examining the snapshot. It was not a particularly good one; there was a certain fuzziness about the outline, as though the camera had moved or the lens had not been properly in focus. But there was no mistaking Clare. She was holding a tennis racket; perhaps the photograph had been taken during that party about which she had written in her last letter; possibly Harry Loader had brought his camera.

Even in a black-and-white photograph the sun-tan was apparent on Clare's face and arms and legs, her hair bleached by sunlight. No one would have had to be told that she spent much of her time in the open air; there was no city pallor about her. She was tall — even Mason did not overtop her by more than three inches — and her body was in perfect proportion to its height; there was no heaviness, no awkwardness in her movements.

Mason thought of this as he stared at the photograph. He remembered all the attraction of Clare. He remembered also that with no one was he so much at ease as he was with her. When they played tennis together their game seemed to dovetail as if by instinct rather than by design, so that at times there seemed to be so deep an understanding between them that words were not necessary. It was as though between their minds there was an absolute and altogether satisfying harmony.

And, despite all that, there remained Jo.

Mason read the letter carefully. It brought everything of that other world to him as if he had been carried back on a magic carpet. And it was another world — so different from that in which he was living at the moment that the two seemed to have no connexion. In Clare's world were tennis-parties and cricket-matches, discussion of crops and livestock, days at market, tinkering with cars and tractors, horse-riding, dances — the pursuits of peace. In this world were guns and sea-sickness, the threat of torpedo and bomb, discomfort, dirt, sudden death — and Jo. The two were apart, separate, bearing so little resemblance that when he passed from one to the other it was as though he became a different person. These were the two halves of his life — the half of peace and the half of war; in the one was Clare and in the other Jo.

He would have liked to tell Clare about Jo, but he knew that that was impossible. To Clare people like Jo did not even exist. He had not the command of words to make her exist, and he knew that it would be a mistake to try. Yet he would have liked to confide in Clare. He had always done so in the past. But this one thing he must keep from her, and how it would turn out he could not tell.

He began to write an answer to the letter: 'My dearest Clare, — We have been rather busy these last few days and I have had not time to write . . . ' It was like a business report. But what else could he say? Nothing except the things that were not important.

When he had written a page he got up and stood looking out of the chart-room window. He saw a crane swinging another load of ammunition across from the quay. The arm of the crane halted above the hold and the load dropped smoothly, disappearing from sight below the level of the coaming. An empty tray came up, hooked by two corners so that it hung perpendicular like an inn sign, swung across to the quay, dropped and was unhooked. The process seemed endless, monotonous, the crane moving as if it were endowed with a brain, a brain that told it when to stop and when to rise, when to swivel and when to remain still. And gradually the ship settled deeper in the water as the weight of shells and hand-grenades and cordite and cartridges grew in her holds.

Mason wondered how long the ship would take to load. How many more days before they sailed again for the beaches? How many more hours with Jo?

★ ★ ★

He could feel the girl tremble when the bomb exploded. He wondered how close it was. The house shook; the windows vibrated; there was a sound of something dropping to the floor — perhaps a little plaster from the ceiling.

"It's all right," he said. "All right."

They had heard the bomb go over, the chatter of its engine, and the ominous silence preceding the explosion. How near had it been? It was difficult to tell. Near enough.

"You're not scared?" he asked.

"Yes," she said, "I'm always scared of bombs. It wouldn't be so bad if you could be sure of being killed at once. Bang — out — just like that, so that you knew nothing about it. It's the idea of being half-killed — having an arm torn off — a leg — being blinded . . . "

"Don't think about it."

"But I have to think about it. I'm scared."

"Everybody is scared."

"Not everybody. You're not."

"How do you know? You can't tell what goes on inside somebody else's mind. A man could be scared out of his wits and nobody know. He'll hide it, you see, because he'd be ashamed to show his fear."

"Have you been afraid — often?"

"Too often."

The day was coming — a dim light creeping into the room, gradually hardening the lines of the bits and pieces of furniture. Mason was silent, thinking back to times of fear — fear so powerful that it had seemed to freeze the limbs.

There had been such a time in the winter of 1942, somewhere off North Cape, in the Arctic Ocean — Heinkel bombers coming in one after another, a tanker in flames, an ammunition ship cracking open like the Day of

262

Judgment. He had wanted to run then, find somewhere to hide his head. There was ice on the sea, and the wind was like a river of ice flowing over the ship. But it was not the wind that made him cold, it was the fear — the fear as they waited, with the gun following the plane that was coming in to attack them, following it but not yet firing, waiting for the range to close.

He wanted to run; and perhaps he would have run, would have disgraced himself, if it had not been for Platt. Platt was standing there with a clip of shells in his hands, his face expressionless, not moving, not moving hand or foot, waiting as calmly as if he had been waiting for a bus. It braced Mason. If Platt was not scared, then why should he be? He was damned if he would be a lesser man than Platt, who had been nothing but an auctioneer's clerk before joining the Army. So he stayed with the gun, and when the shells began blasting out of the longbarrel his fear left him, because then there was no time for fear. It was only later that he rememberd it, talking to Platt. And he remembered now what

Platt had said: 'I wanted to run, but I had those shells in my hands, and I was so bloody paralysed with fright that I just couldn't think what to do with them. So I stayed there. But if it hadn't been for those shells I reckon I'd have gone.'

Platt — poor, unlucky Platt, who had bought it somewhere on the long haul from Cape Town to Sydney.

"I should have said you didn't know what fear was," Jo said.

"If a man doesn't know that, then there's something wrong with him."

"But you're not a coward."

"It's not the same thing. There's many a man would be a coward if he dared."

"I don't think I understand that."

"No?" He turned and looked at her. Her face seemed grey in the half-light of the early morning. "It doesn't matter. Maybe there's no sense in it anyway. Maybe there's no sense in anything any more."

"There's sense in us — you and me. We don't have to think of anything else — not bombs nor nothing — just ourselves. While it lasts."

"You don't have to think about its ending, Jo."

"But it will end just the same. How soon?"

"Perhaps not ever, Jo. Not as long as we live."

"That's nonsense. You know it is."

"No." At this hour in the morning you got queer ideas into your head. Ideas like being married to Jo. But an idea like that never went any further. If you tried to picture Jo living in the country, being a farmer's wife, it just seemed absurd, about as likely as making a mermaid into a housewife. And yet he loved Jo and wanted to keep her always.

"I hate the light," she said. "I wish the morning would never come. I wish the night would last for ever."

"But I like to see you, Jo. I like to look at you."

"I look better in the dark," she said.

He could see the bones of her cheeks pressing up through the skin. A fringe of hair had fallen down over her forehead. He smoothed it away with his hand. He kissed her throat, and felt her pulse throbbing under his lips.

10

Week-end in June

"WE shall be in dock over the week-end," Captain Garner said. "I thought you'd like to know, sergeant."

Mason thanked him for the information. "I wasn't expecting it. I thought the cargo would be loaded."

"It's not a question of cargo. There's a job on the engines that won't be finished. You might like to take a trip home if it's not too far. I could give you a pass."

"Hardly time for that, sir. But I'd be glad of the pass. I've got friends in London."

"All right, then. You might see whether any of the others want to get away. Just so long as one stays on board."

Garner had a pen in his hand and a pair of spectacles perched on his nose. They altered the whole appearance of his face; seemed to make it altogether more benevolent, less dominated by the scarred lip and the thrusting chin. Wearing glasses, he seemed in a way to have become suddenly clerk-like, domesticated, the pirate in him thrust into the background. But the hands did not fit the rôle of clerk; they were too massive, too thickly covered with black hairs. In those muscular, stubby fingers the pen was as out of place as it would have been in the hand of a gorilla. And yet his writing, small, neat, regular, and perfectly legible, would not have discredited the most fastidious of book-keepers.

Lying on the table in front of him Mason could see the violin. It seemed to have been repaired with more than average skill, and he wondered whether Garner was one of those seamen whose manual dexterity is sometimes reflected in models of full-rigged ships, accurate to the smallest detail of topsail-yard and spanker-boom, of monkey-gaff and futtock-shroud. He had once seen an old bosun, equipped only with a sailor's clasp-knife, carving wooden dolls with a delicacy of touch that a sculptor might have envied. And the man had thought nothing of it; it had been a mere pastime, a hobby to while away an idle hour on a long sea-voyage. He had known a carpenter, a big Orcadian speaking a language that could hardly be described as English, who made exquisite pastel drawings of ships and seascapes and foreign harbours, and gave them away to anyone who might express a desire to have them.

"The violin all right now?" he asked. It was a tactless question, but Garner showed no resentment. He seemed now to be able to look back upon the revels that had led to the damage as a man looks back to the follies of his youth — with a smile of indulgence.

"As good as ever. It's not the first time it's needed a bit of patching up here and there. That old fiddle has seen some things in its time. I reckon if it could speak it'd have a tale to tell. Not that it's valuable or anything like that. It's not a Strad or a Guarnerius, you understand; but it's not a bad little instrument — not bad at all."

He rubbed the tips of his fingers along

the smooth, polished wood of the violin as though experiencing some sensuous delight in the contact. Then he said suddenly: "That cook's a liar. He never studied in Milan, you know; all nonsense. Got no voice at all." He pulled some papers towards him. "Well, get along now. I've got work to do."

★ ★ ★

Mason was standing in the doorway of the forecastle when the bomb dropped. He had not heard it coming. There was a winch clattering; perhaps it had drowned any other noise; or perhaps you did not hear the one that was going to hit you, because in that case you were at the end of the silent, slanting dive that followed when the motor cut out. This bomb did not hit the ship, but it was so close that the blast made the derricks vibrate, and the ship itself shuddered as though a shock-wave had passed along the dock; to communicate with the iron hull and the lethal cargo that it contained.

The explosion set Mason's ears singing; the drums seemed to be sucked out and then thrust in again with a click. He heard something drop, tinkling, to the deck at his feet. He picked it up and saw that it was a piece of grey metal, very light, twisted and curled like the leaf of a Savoy cabbage.

Gates came tumbling out of the cabin, and he showed the fragment to him. "A piece of a doodle-bug," he said.

Gates looked at it with interest, took it in his hand, and weighed it. "That stuff wouldn't do much harm to a brick wall. It's too light. So it must be the blast that does it." He gave the metal back to Mason and stepped out on to the deck. "Some people seem to be in a hurry," he said.

The winch had stopped, the cranes were motionless. After the sudden bursting of the bomb a silence had fallen on the ship, broken only by the scamper of men's feet as the dockers came up out of the holds and scattered.

"A bit late for that sort of thing," Gates said. "Do they expect another one to fall in the same place?"

"God knows what they expect," Mason said. "They've got the wind up — that's all." He went to the edge of the hatch and looked down into the hold. It was already more than half full — the shells, the tubes of cordite, the boxes of ammunition stacked away neatly and tightly, so that however much the ship might pitch or roll, none of the cargo could come adrift. Bits of dunnage separated the layers, and filled up the spaces where the shape of the sides made spaces unavoidable. It occurred to Mason that men who had had no practice in this sort of job could make an awful mess of it — a mess that might well mean the loss of a ship.

And now, because of the coming of the bomb, all this work had suddenly come to a stop. How suddenly was shown by the fact that a tray of 5.5-inch shells lay on top of the cargo, half emptied, a man's jacket hung from a bolt, a half-eaten sandwich rested on an ammunition-box, a sheet of newspaper by its side, and the hook from the crane, with its massive weight like the bob on a plumb-line, still dangled, swinging slightly from side to side, in the middle of the hatch. It was like the setting for one of those mysteries of the sea — a

271

ship deserted by its crew for no apparent reason. But here the reason was known — the sudden panic caused by the dropping of a bomb close by, and the knowledge that this cargo on which they were working could itself go up in a mountain of flame and smoke and jagged metal.

"I suppose they'll come back," Mason said.

Gates thought it likely. "Leave them alone and they'll come home and bring their tails behind them."

They drifted back slowly — in twos and threes, looking sheepish. Gradually the work started again, but they were nervous — each man kept an ear cocked for the sound of a flying-bomb, giving only half his mind to his work, and the other half to that winged peril in the skies.

"I wonder how many that one killed," Gates said.

There, Mason thought, was the queer part about it: the bomb must have been so near, near enough to throw a piece of metal on to the deck of the *Radgate*; and yet, separated from them by walls and buildings, it might have been in another country. They could not even see what damage it had caused. But for the sudden shock, the brief cessation of work, the period of awed silence, it had affected them not at all. Yet a few yards difference in its range and there would have been no question of a week-end with Jo.

★ ★ ★

Kids were playing on the bombed site when he reached the house on the Saturday afternoon. A man in shirt-sleeves with a navvy's belt round his waist cannoned into him as he was about to go through the doorway. "Sorry, mate." He looked at Mason without curiosity, accepting him as part of the landscape. "Nice weather." He went off down the street, rolling slightly, as though he were partly drunk or had just come from the sea.

Mason went in, and the odour of the house met him like a wave. A woman was climbing the stairs, a fat, wheezing, elderly woman, making slow progress.

Mason, wanting to run, was forced to match his pace to hers.

She heard him coming up behind her, and began to complain cheerfully: "These stairs'll be the death of me. Too much weight to carry and not enough strength to carry it — that's my trouble."

"Never mind," Mason said. "Take it easy."

The woman rested with one hand on the banisters and looked down at him. Her hair was white in streaks like a badger's head; it hung down in untidy wisps on either side of her sagging face. She appeared to be short-sighted, for she screwed up her eyes as if to bring Mason into focus.

"When I was your age I'd 'ave gone up these stairs like a bird. You'd 'ave 'ad a job to catch me then — so you would."

Mason laughed. He was in a happy mood. "You think I'd have wanted to catch you?"

"No doubt you would, boy. All the lads was after me in them days. Well, well, you're only young once. You want to make the most of it. That's what I say."

"Let me give you hand up," Mason said.

She shook her head. "No, no. I'm all right. Never mind about me." She winked — slowly, ponderously. "You go and enjoy yourself. I'll say this — you're a fine-looking boy. Wish I was forty years younger. I'd set my cap at you."

"Get along with you," Mason said, and went up the stairs past her, wondering how much she knew about him — and how much she knew about Jo. She might have been able to tell him things he would rather not hear; she looked the sort who would not need much encouragement to gossip. Well, he was not going to encourage her. He had a distrust of all the other people who lived in the house. He wished they were not there — men and women, all of them, he distrusted them. And that door to Jo's room without a lock.

She was not there when he went in, but there was a note lying on the table: 'Be back soon. Jo.' It was written in pencil on a piece of cardboard torn from a soap-flake packet. It was the first time he had seen her handwriting, and he examined it with interest as a new side to her character. In fact there was little enough character in the big, scrawling letters. He would not have expected her to write like that; and yet when he came to think about it he had to admit to himself that a neat, tidy hand would not have matched the ways of the girl. She, impatient of discipline, of convention, would not have applied herself patiently to the production of anything so controlled, so decorous.

He was still looking at the cardboard when she came in. She had a string bag in her hand, and she was breathing rapidly, as though she had been running. There was a flush of colour in her usually pale cheeks.

"I wondered whether you'd be here. Have you been waiting long?"

He held up the cardboard. "Just long enough to read your note."

"Oh, that's all right then. I hurried."

She put the bag on the table, and came to him, lifting up her face to be kissed in the way that he had come to associate with her — like a child begging for sweets.

276

"You've been running?"

"Yes — all the way."

"Where've you been?"

"Shopping. I have to eat, you know."

"I don't think you eat enough."

"Well, that's the fault of the system, isn't it? Rations for one don't come to a lot."

"I know — not half enough. But I've brought something." He picked up the haversack that he had dropped when he came into the room and began to unload it on to the table. "Bacon, cheese, bully-beef, condensed milk, chocolate, tea, cigarettes."

She looked at him in amazement. "How'd you manage to get all this?"

"Influence," Mason said. But it had taken some powers of persuasion. The cook had not been in a good mood. He was still suffering from the effects of his argument with the fireman; his lips were puffed up, and there was a piece of sticking-plaster on one cheek. He was unshaven and untidy as ever, and his eye was bloodshot — a basilisk eye that peered angrily from beneath a ragged curtain of eyebrow.

"Rations!" the cook said. "What do you mean — rations? You get no rations out of me."

Mason was patient, stepping delicately on treacherous ground. "I shall be ashore over the week-end, don't you see? I shan't be eating on board, so it should be all right if I take my grub with me."

"Rations," the cook said, laying down the laws, "is for consumption *in situ* — on the site — on board ship — here. No off licence."

He had made a joke, and Mason laughed tactfully. "Of course," he said. "I know all about regulations. But regulations are made for small-minded persons; isn't that so?"

The cook said nothing, but scratched his stomach with the handle of a ladle. There was a wide hole in his singlet which allowed him to get really down to the heart of the work. The ladle made a sound like a farmer's stick scratching the back of a pig.

"Regulations," Mason continued, warming to the subject, "are not meant to be taken literally except by petty officials whose minds are too mean to allow them any freedom of action. Large-minded people — such people as yourself, for example — would interpret the law as it is meant to be interpreted."

The cook reversed the ladle and began to scratch the inaccessible regions of his back. He still said nothing. He stared at Mason, waiting for him to go on. They were alone in the galley, which was a hot, cramped deckhouse just aft of the bridge, having a sink and a bench on one side, an iron cooking-stove and a coal-bunker on the other, with a narrow passage between connecting doorways on the port and starboard sides.

"A man like you," Mason said, "with all your vast experience of the world, must be large-minded; it stands to reason. A man who has studied singing in Milan, who has cooked for royalty, is, I should say, hardly likely to feel himself bound hand and foot by pettifogging regulations formulated by some snotty-nosed clerk shining his arse on a stool in Whitehall. There are some cooks, no doubt, who would be afraid to bend the law to the needs of humanity, scared of possible consequences. I've known some — bad cooks, too, who'd give you sea-pie for three days of the week and scouse for the rest of the time — "

"Liverpool bastards — never were no good." The cook was a Southampton man.

"That's it," Mason said, striking the hot iron. "You wouldn't expect any decency from such as them. But you, if I may say so, are an entirely different kettle of fish. After all, a man who has studied singing under Toscanini — "

"Gordini."

"Just so — Gordini. A man who has been distiller-in-chief to the Sultan of — where was it?"

The cook grinned suddenly. "Okay. You don't have to go on. I reckon you've earned a few rations. Talking like that — you ought to be a lawyer. Well, what is it you want? Bacon, cheese . . . "

Having been won over, the cook had been generous — the bacon alone would have made up six weeks' ration for a civilian.

"Don't go gabbing about it," he said. "I don't want everybody crowding me. Keep it dark, see? Just keep it dark."

"You can trust me," Mason said.

"I don't trust nobody; never did. I'm no fool."

When Mason left him he was sitting on the floury cooking-board and picking his teeth with a skewer. He seemed to have relapsed once more into a gloomy, introspective mood, perhaps dwelling upon the glories of the past and comparing them with the dismal sordidness of the present.

★ ★ ★

Jo was in high spirits. "A whole week-end. Nothing to do but please ourselves. You don't have to go back Sunday evening, do you? Nothing silly like that?"

"Not on your life. Not until Monday morning." He looked at his wrist-watch, calculating. "Forty-one hours and fourteen minutes. What shall we do this afternoon?"

"Go swimming."

"You'd like that?"

"Please."

"Swimming it is, then."

Going down the stairs with Jo, it

occurred to Mason that this was the first time he had left the house with her. On the first evening she had taken him there and he had followed her, but all the other times he had come and gone by himself. Going out with her gave him a sense of possession; he did not try to analyse the feeling, he just accepted it.

There was a week-end throb of activity in the house. It was as though behind every door people were relaxing in a brief freedom from labour — playing gramphones, cooking meals, throwing crockery, shouting at one another, getting ready to go out and enjoy themselves as much as one could in a city menaced by flying-bombs and depressed by wartime scarcities.

A boy was standing in the ground-floor doorway, throwing stones across the street. He stared as Mason pushed by.

"You got a gun, sergeant?" he asked.

"Not on me."

"My big brother's got a gun what'll stop a tank."

"That's quite a gun," Mason said.

The swimming-bath was in a big, old-fashioned building faced with glazed tiles.

Although the sun was shining outside, the interior was gloomy, the light filtered by dirty glass, the strength taken out of it. A continuous noise, echoing hollowly in the high-domed structure, turned out to be the massed voices of dozens of boys and girls who were enjoying themselves vigorously in the water.

"Looks pretty full," Mason said.

"It's always like this on Saturdays. There'll be room for us."

Mason went to a cubicle and changed quickly, but when he came out Jo was already in the water. She came up the ladder from the deep end, smiling, her hair dripping.

"I love swimming."

He thought she looked thinner than ever in the blue bathing-suit. She put a wet hand on his arm. "Come on in."

"You first. I'll catch you."

"Try."

She dived with scarcely a splash, slipping away underwater like a seal. Mason thrust with his feet on the side of the bath and did a racing dive. He caught her half-way across, gripped her wrist, and pulled her round to face him.

"Hi, mermaid. What's the hurry?"

She laughed at him, the water dripping from her face, happy. "So you can swim. I wondered whether you could. You didn't tell me."

He wondered whether it had been some kind of test. If so he had passed it. She might be more agile in the water than he; she might dive better, but he could beat her for speed.

He released her wrist, and she dived under him. He went down after her, put his arm round her waist, and pulled her to him under water. They both came up gasping for breath. Mason could see the laughter in her eyes, the joy of living. It was going to be a good week-end.

★ ★ ★

That evening they stood and watched while three flying-bombs in quick succession rattled overhead. They were at a point high up from which they could see a great sweep of London, stretching away like a jumble of dolls' houses, with here and there the tall chimney of a factory thrusting up from the pile, or the spire of a church. Into that jumble the bombs glided down. A flash, dust rising in the air, a distant rumble as of a single clap of thunder — and that was all.

They were standing on a viaduct, close together against the iron parapet, and below them railway-lines gleamed like silver ribbons; an engine shunted past, puffing up balls of smoke and steam. Mason watched the third bomb explode. Half a mile away? A mile? It was difficult to tell

"I wonder what part that is," he said.

"I don't know," Jo said. "I don't want to know."

She was right, Mason thought. As long as you did not know you could feel only an impersonal interest in the matter. The bomb had fallen; you knew that houses had been blown down, people killed, maimed; but it was too far away to be any of your business. You could not do anything to help; you were powerless to divert the bomb, and you were powerless to aid the injured. You were like a spectator at some play — you saw everything happening, you were interested, but you were not personally involved.

In a way this living in London with the flying-bombs coming over was like taking part in a lottery. If you drew the lucky number you missed being hit; if you were unlucky it was just too bad; but you could do nothing about it. These things were coming over day and night; it was impossible to spend all your time in a shelter.

When they had watched the third bomb Jo pulled at Mason's sleeve. "Let's go."

"Scared?" he asked.

She answered the question after due consideration: "No. Not out here. Not with you. It's when I'm alone in the house I get frightened. I think of it all collapsing on top of me. That's when I'm scared."

"When I'm away you must sleep in the shelter."

"I may do that. But I hate shelters."

"Better than being killed. You want to live, don't you?"

"Of course I want to live. I love life."

He could believe it. The joy of living

was like a pulse beating inside her. He could not imagine her dead. Hers was a kind of life force that had to go on. He could not imagine her old, either. She had to be always just as she was now, at this single moment of time, with all the magnetism of youth that drew him to her. If he tried to look into the future to see what there was in it for him and Jo he saw only a blank. The imagination was not strong enough to picture how it might be — Jo growing old beside him, the energy, the gaiety, dying out of her. He could not and would not see it. He wanted her to remain always like this — a kind of spirit, a flame burning at the heart of all this death and destruction, a flame that should prove unquenchable. Perhaps that was what she was to him — a symbol of life amid death; perhaps that was why he loved her and could not imagine her any older, any different from what she was now.

"We'll buy some fish-and-chips," she said. "I'm hungry."

She had broken the web of his thoughts with an earthy hand. He laughed — at her and at himself. "I'm hungry too."

They ate the fish-and-chips from a newspaper as they walked back to the house — and they tasted good. What did it matter where you ate your food when you were hungry? Picking it out of a newspaper with your fingers, it was still good.

They stopped at a public house, and he fought his way to the bar to fetch a glass of gin for Jo and a pint of beer for himself. The beer was warm and flat, but it quenched his thirst. Neither he nor Jo had any inclination to stay for a second drink. It was not the house in which he had first met her, but the atmosphere made him think of Dave, of that brief encounter on the pavement. He did not want to see Dave again — ever.

"Let's go," he said.

★ ★ ★

The house woke slowly in the morning. Mason, half asleep, heard somebody go past in the corridor. Then there was a long silence during which he dozed again, only to be reawakened by a sudden heavy thump on the floor above. The room faced east, and there was a patch of sunlight on the floor; a spider scampered across it, stealthily, like a murderer fleeing from the scene of his crime. Mason reached out a hand for his battledress blouse, took a cigarette, and lit it. He lay back on the pillow, smoking, watching the smoke drift up towards the ceiling, feeling lazy, luxuriating in the knowledge that he did not have to go back to the ship until Monday. Nearly twenty-four hours more of freedom.

Jo awoke and demanded a cigarette. He lit it for her, kissed her, and put the cigarette between her lips.

"Where do you want to go today?"

"Into the country."

"The country? You mean that?"

"Why shouldn't I? I'm sick of this filthy town. I want to get away from the bricks and the mortar. Breathe some fresh air."

Mason was surprised. He would not have supposed the country would have held any attraction for her. But he was glad.

"All right, then. That's what we'll do."

They caught a train at Liverpool

Street Station and travelled in a carriage crammed to suffocation with soldiers. Somewhere beyond Bishop's Stortford they left the train and walked.

To Mason the sight of cornfields and meadows was like a glimpse of home. He wondered how Jo was reacting to this scene, so different from her normal outlook. He told her which fields were barley, which wheat, which oats. It was a distinction so simple that it had never occurred to him that anyone could be ignorant of it.

"How do you know?" she asked.

"By the look of them."

"They all look alike to me."

"You'll learn the difference one day."

"Shall I? I don't think so." She looked at him suddenly, almost accusingly. "This is your world, isn't it? This is where you belong."

Mason grinned. "Not this part. Farther north. But you're breaking the contract. We agreed not to pry into each other's business, didn't we?"

"I'm not prying. I don't care where you live — what you are — anything. I don't want to know."

She seemed suddenly out of humour. Mason was puzzled by her change of mood. It had been she who had suggested coming into the country; but now that they were here she seemed depressed. He felt, too, that she was watching him, weighing something up in her mind; though what it was he could not guess. Her long silences, her thoughtfulness, were unusual. He tried to rally her, but without success. Finally he became depressed also.

When it began to rain they decided to go back.

11

A Visitor

IT was almost dark when they arrived back at the house. Jo went into the room first, and Mason heard her give a little cry that died away at once. He followed her in and closed the door behind him. Jo had moved only a yard or two past the threshold, and Mason could see behind her, outlined against the last glow of daylight from the window, the figure of a man.

The man said: "So you've come back at last. I bin waiting a long time." His voice was hoarse, rather wheezy, as though he smoked too many cigarettes.

"You!" Jo said. "What do you want?"

"Help, Josie. Just a bit of help. That's all."

Jo went to the window and put up the black-out board. "Switch the light on, Peter," she said.

Mason did so, and saw who the man

was. It was the deserter who had broken into the room when the military police were hunting him. He was in uniform now, but the uniform failed to make a soldier of him. His battledress blouse was unbuttoned, hanging loose; his hair was ruffled. He looked pale and ill.

"What sort of help?" Jo asked.

The man looked at Mason and nodded, recognizing him. "Evening, sergeant. My name's Watts — Henry Watts. Private in His Majesty's Forces. Unwilling." He turned to Jo, and there was a trace of iron in his voice. "Financial help — that's what. A bit of money to see me on my way. You don't want me staying here, do you? That wouldn't suit, would it?"

She turned on him with a burst of anger that surprised Mason. "What makes you think I'd let you do that anyway? Stay here! You're not staying here, I can tell you that. Why, you fool, isn't this the place they'll come looking for you?"

"I know that, Josie. That's why I got to have money — so's I can get away."

Mason said coldly: "You've deserted again, then?"

Watts put a finger to this nose. "Let's

not say anything about that, shall we? Least said, soonest mended. Ain't that so? No need to put words to acts."

In spite of his miserable appearance, his worn, haggard features, his round shoulders, his thin, untidy hair, there was a certain air of mastery about the man. It was as though he knew that he had some power that he could use if necessary. He jerked a thumb at Jo, and leered at Mason.

"How much do you know about her, sergeant? Would you like to know something? Should I give you some information?"

Jo broke in: "How much do you want?"

He seemed to consider, perhaps wondering just how much he could draw. "Shall we say ten quid? It ain't much, but it'll get me on my way. That's what you want, ain't it? To get rid of me."

"Ten pounds! Where do you think I'd find that much money? Talk sense."

"I am talking sense — real sense." He gripped Jo's wrist suddenly. He was more arrogant than he had been the last time

Mason had seen him. His breath smelled of spirits, and it was likely that this was where his courage originated. "You come across, see?"

Mason said sharply: "Let go her wrist."

Watts let go quickly. His courage was obviously not unlimited, however it might have been obtained.

Jo said: "I'll give you two pounds — that's all. I can't give you any more. I haven't got it to give. You take two pounds and get out of here quick."

Watts sat down on a chair and crossed his legs. "Two quid's no good at all. You ought to know that."

"And what's the use of ten either? Where will that get you? Where'll you go?"

"Don't you worry your head about that, me girl. That's my worry. I've got a place to go; but I got to have money."

"Well, I haven't got it — and that's that."

"Maybe the sergeant here would help. What d'you say, sergeant?"

"You're a deserter," Mason said. "I ought to pull you in." That was, of course, his duty. But he knew — and Watts knew too — that he would not carry out that duty. He wanted no trouble with the military police. He wondered what hold this man had over Jo. And yet he did not wish to know; he wanted to know nothing about it. He wanted, as Jo did, to get rid of Watts and forget that he even existed.

"All right," Watts said. "You pull me in. I don't set myself up as being strong enough to fight you. But before we start any rough stuff let's have a nice cosy talk, shall we? Let's swap a few life-stories — yours, mine, hers."

"You shut your mouth," Jo said. "We don't want any lies out of you."

"Lies, is it? Well, maybe so and maybe not so. That'd be for the sergeant to decide, wouldn't it? I wonder how much you've told him. Have you shared all your secrets? Let me see; it's just a fortnight since he first came here. I don't know where you picked him up. I'm not asking. But I notice things. I got eyes in my head, and I use 'em. I'm not a fool — not Henry Watts — not this boy."

"That's just what you are — a damned fool."

Watts did not appear to be put out. His calmness was a contrast to Jo's anger. He seemed to feel that he had the situation well in hand.

"Maybe I am; but that's neither here nor there. The point is — do I get my ten quid or don't I?"

"I told you I haven't got that much money."

Watt's gaze shifted from her to Mason. His expression made him look wolfish. "Are you in love with this soldier-boy, Josie?"

"What do you know about love?"

"And you called me a fool. I'm surprised at you. I thought you knew better. Now, if anyone had asked me I'd have said you were too clever. Josie, I'd have said, why she — "

She struck him across the mouth with the back of her hand, and the sound was startlingly loud in the close and stifling room. It stopped Watt's flow of speech. He sat there, rubbing his mouth and staring at Jo with venomous eyes.

"You little bitch."

"Cut it out," Mason said. "Start talking like that and you'll find yourself pitched down the stairs."

"That would be smart, wouldn't it? I suppose you think you're in love with her too. You're a pair, ain't you? Kids! When you're as old as I am . . . But maybe you never will be — not neither of you. Let me tell you a story — "

"I don't want to hear any of your stories."

"No? It might be instructive. You might draw some useful morals."

"A fine set of morals. I've no doubt."

"According to taste. There's morals and morals . . . "

"Here. Take this and go," Jo said. She was holding three pound-notes under Watt's nose. "It's all I've got. If you make any trouble you won't get that amount. Coming in here like this as if you had the right — "

Watts grabbed the money and stuffed it in his pocket. "As if I had the right, hey? Well, we'll let that one pass. Three quid. It ain't much. I don't know as how — "

"Look," Mason said. "You'd better get

out of here before something unpleasant happens to you."

Watts's face took on a obstinate expression. "Three quid ain't enough. I tell you — "

"It'll have to be enough. Are you getting up out of that chair or do I have to drag you up?"

Watts sat more firmly where he was. "Threats won't get you nowhere, sergeant. We ain't on parade now. You might bribe me to go. I don't say I'd be above taking a bribe. But I won't be forced."

Mason's patience was wearing thin. He wanted to get Watts out of the room — out of the house. There was a feeling of uncleanliness with him sitting there. It was as if a canker had settled at the heart of the room, at the heart of his relations with Jo. He still did not know who this man was; he knew his name, and that was all. If the truth were told he did not wish to know; was indeed afraid to know more. He wanted to get rid of him — quickly — before he started talking again.

"You're coming now." He stooped and

seized the collar of Watts's battledress blouse, dragging him to his feet. Watts came suddenly, viciously active, like a snake that has been disturbed in the grass. He kicked hard at Mason's shins, and Mason let go. Watts moved to the sink and whipped up a bread-knife that had been lying on the draining-board. He held it thrust out in front of him, daring Mason to advance. There was an evil expression on his face.

"You try any tricks, me lad, and you get this in your face. Spoil your nice looks, it would. Try pitching me out — come on — try. See how you like it."

Mason made a move towards him and the knife flashed out like a steel tongue — warningly. Mason stopped. There was no doubt that Watts meant what he said. He was not making idle threats.

Jo said quickly, urgently: "Don't do it, Peter. He'll use the knife. I know him."

Watts laughed. He seemed to be enjoying himself. "Right enough she knows me. My God, she ought to."

"Put that knife down," Jo said. "I'll

give you another two pounds — and that really is all I've got. But put the knife down."

Watts continued to hold the knife. "Two pounds more, eh? Well, well; that's getting better. If I hold out a bit longer we might get up to the ten quid what I asked for in the first place, mightn't we?"

"Don't give him any more, Jo," Mason said.

Watts snarled at him: "You don't tell her what to do. I do the telling — see? You ask her if that's not right."

"Is it right, Jo?" Mason asked.

"No."

Watts sneered. "You think not? All right, then; you tell him who I am. Tell him about us, Josie — you and me. Tell him about the games we've played together. Kids' games, eh, Josie? Tell him — "

He had turned his attention to the girl, and his eyes had shifted their vigilance from Mason. Mason took the opportunity without hesitation. His fist crashed into Watts's jaw, and Watts went backward like a jolted punch-bag. His head struck the edge of the sink and he fell to the floor, the knife clattering from his hand.

Mason sucked his knuckles. "The damned little swine. Threatening me — "

Watts lay where he had fallen, not moving.

"You hit him hard," Jo said.

"He asked for it."

They refused at first to believe that Watts was dead. They tried to believe that he was only unconscious. There was no blood; and only the smallest evidence of a blow at the base of the skull where it had come into contact with the hard porcelain of the sink. But he was dead. They stared at each other in horror as the realization came to them.

"What do we do now?" Jo asked. "Oh, Peter, what do we do now?"

"We'll think of something," he said. But his brain was racing. Think of something! Yes — he must think of something; and think quickly.

"You'd better tell me about him," he said, and his voice was harsh. "I'd better hear it all now. You tell me and then I'll think."

"There's not a lot to tell — not really.

He was a bad man — bad all through. I'm not sorry he's dead. He'd have been better dead years ago."

"I know he was bad. What I want to know is what you had to do with him." He had to hear it now. It was no use trying to be blind any longer. Not with the dead man lying there at his feet. He pulled a blanket off the bed and put it over Watts, blotting out the sight of evil.

Jo said: "Give me a cigarette, Peter. I need one."

Her hand was trembling when she took it from him. He lit one for himself. He needed it too. What was he going to do with Watts? He had to think of something.

"He took me when I was young," Jo said. "I was no more than a kid — just out of the orphanage — doing domestic work. He was smarter then — in his appearance. Good-looking too, though you mightn't believe it. He had a way with him, and he said he was out to help me. Him — he never helped anybody but himself. I believed him. I was green. I didn't find out until later that he was a criminal — that he'd been in gaol; and by that time he'd got a hold over me that I didn't know how to break. I had a job in a big house. The woman was rich, lazy, easy-going. She left things lying about — jewellery. I didn't take anything myself, but I helped Harry, and he did the taking. After that we moved around, working together — me on the inside. I hated it; you don't know how I hated it. I wanted to be like other people, and I couldn't. He'd got me and he wasn't letting me go. I was too useful to him — much too useful."

Mason sucked smoke into his lungs and looked at the blanket-covered heap on the floor. He felt no remorse. The impression of guilt was completely lacking. He did not even feel that he had murdered a man. It had been an accident; but Watts was better out of the way. He had been a parasite, sucking a living out of the society to which he refused to give any service in return. Certainly he would be no loss. The problem was how to get rid of the body.

"There were other things," Jo said

almost in a whisper, "worse things — "

"I don't want to hear any more," Mason said. He felt only compassion for the girl — compassion and love. He did not blame her; he blamed only the dead man. "It wasn't your fault."

She answered almost fiercely, repudiating that exoneration: "It was — it was. I was a fool. I thought I knew all the answers, and I didn't know one — not a single one. It wasn't till the Army took him that I got away. But he found me. You see he found me."

The tears began to come then — flowing silently. And Mason was glad that she could find this emotional relief. He put his arm round her shoulders, thinking again how slight they were to bear the burden of so many problems. He tried to comfort her. "There'll be a way out, Jo. This isn't the end — not for you and me. It might be a new beginning. There's sure to be a way out."

And all the while his brain working feverishly — searching for that way.

★ ★ ★

Jo went down the stairs first, and Mason followed with Watts's body slung over his shoulder like a long, thin sack. They met no one in the house; it was silent, sleeping. And yet, following the trail of the torch that Jo was holding, Mason had the feeling that from beyond the edges of the light eyes were watching him, taking note of his movements. The rotten odour of the house oppressed him more than it had ever done before: this was the odour of decay and death, and this was death that he carried on his shoulder. Watts was not heavy; he was no great weight to carry; and yet Mason felt as though he had upon his back the Old Man of the Sea, of whom he would never again be able to rid himself.

He was glad when they came out into the street, into the freshness of the night air. He told Jo to go on ahead, and he would follow her. "We don't want to be together. It would look more suspicious."

She did as she was told, moving off up the street, and Mason followed with the burden on his shoulder, following the occasional flashes of the torch that dropped like little pools of light on to the pavement.

He had gone perhaps a quarter of a mile when the policeman stopped him. The policemen's torch bored a hole in the darkness, spotlighting his face.

"Now what's this?" the policeman asked.

"My mate's drunk," Mason said. "I'm taking him back to the billet."

The statement came out without hesitation. He had rehearsed it beforehand. He was surprised to find that his voice was quite steady.

"You look hot," the policeman said, still keeping the torch shining on Mason's face, where the sweat was streaming down. "Is he heavy?"

"Not too heavy," Mason said. "I'll manage."

"Sure he isn't dead?" The policeman laughed. Mason could see only a vague shadow beyond the gleam of the torch, but the man sounded good-natured. His laugh was like the laugh of a fat, comfortable man. Mason joined in the laughter, forcing himself to do so.

"Nothing like that," he said. "I've had

this trouble with him before. Can't take his liquor."

"There's some like that," the policeman said. He moved the torch-beam to Watts head, and Mason was thankful that he had pulled Watts's beret well down over the mark at the back of the skull. He hoped the beret had not fallen off. The policemen did not appear to be suspicious — just friendly — perhaps glad of the opportunity to talk to some one on a lonely beat. "There's some go flat out on a couple of tots. It's all according to the corpuscles in the blood. Has he had much?"

"No — not a lot."

"Ah, he'll be one of the weak-headed kind. My brother is like that. Gets proper silly on one pint of beer. Wouldn't do for the Force, he wouldn't. But he's a butcher, and that's different. You got far to go?"

"Not very far."

He hoped the policeman would not ask him where the billet was. He did not know the neighbourhood well enough to make a convincing answer. He wondered whether it would be safe to move on, or whether any sign of eagerness might rouse suspicions which were not already in the policeman's head. He was thankful when at last the man switched his torch off and said: "Well, you'd better be getting along. I'd give you a hand at the carrying if I wasn't on duty."

"That's all right," Mason said. "I can manage."

He caught up with Jo at the next corner. Her voice sounded scared. "What did the copper want?"

"He wanted to tell me about his brother who's in the butchery line."

She laughed, with a touch of hysteria.

"Steady," Mason said. "Don't lose your grip."

It had been his idea to dump the body on a bombed site — perhaps hiding it with a pile of rubbish. Jo said she knew a place where there was a cellar that had been revealed by a bomb. If the body were pitched in there it might well be supposed when it was found that Watts had stumbled into the cellar in the black-out and killed himself that way. It was the best plan they could think of.

In the event the plan did not have to

be carried out. Chance produced a better one in the shape of a flying-bomb. Mason heard it coming; he saw the flame in the sky. But he paid no heed to it. He had weightier things on his mind — and on his back. Even when the engine ceased to chatter he did not think that the bomb would fall close enough to affect him. He did not think about it at all. But when the blast threw him off his feet it seemed not to stun him but in fact to quicken the working of his brain, so that he saw in this the complete, the perfect, answer to his problem.

He got to his feet, picked up Watt's body again, and staggered forward into the dust and rubble and darkness ahead. He did not go far; there was no need. He was aware vaguely of noise, of voices shouting, of some one screaming, of a bell clanging, a dog barking. He was aware of dust clogging his nostrils, choking him; of the red flame of a fire; of smoke; of rubble under his stumbling feet. He flung the body down at the base of a wall and turned and ran back the way he had come. He heard the wall falling, crashing down behind him, burying Watts in an avalanche of bricks and mortar, of broken glass and beams.

He found Jo and grabbed her arm, pulling her with him. An ambulance and a fire-engine came racing down the street and they flattened themselves against the wall of a house. Then they ran — ran until the breath burned in their throats — until they could run no farther.

12

On the Beach

"IT'S a good thing you didn't overstay your leave," Captain Garner said. "We're pushing out today."

"Oh," Mason said. He wished there had been another day, so that he could have had one more night ashore before going. Jo had been in a dark mood of depression when he had left her. He supposed she was worrying about Watts. He told her there was no need to worry about that business. It was finished — finished as perfectly as it was possible to finish anything. There would be no repercussions from that.

But Jo had not cheered up. It was as though something else were on her mind also — something that had nothing to do with Watts. It made Mason worried too.

He had told her that if he did not come back that evening he might be away for a week.

"If you don't come back tonight," she said, "you won't come back at all. I shall never see you again."

He had tried to reason with her. "But that's nonsense. Why shouldn't I come back? Nothing's going to stop me. I love you, Jo. You know that."

"Do I? It does not make any difference. If you don't come back tonight I shall never see you again. I know."

He could not shake her out of that belief, though he did his best. When he kissed her good-bye she held him tightly, clasped against her slim, supple body as though she would hold him there for ever. He could feel her trembling, and he knew then that she was really afraid. He wanted to stay with her, but he knew that that was impossible.

He said: "I'll be back tonight," and hoped it was true.

When he had gone half-way down the stairs he turned and ran back again on a sudden impulse. He opened the door softly, and saw her lying on the bed with her face buried in the pillow. He went over to her and put his hand on her shoulder; but without looking up at him she said angrily: "Go away, go away, go away. For God's sake go away and leave me."

He went then, with a troubled mind. He hated to leave her like that, and yet he had to go. It was as though some of her premonition of ill had found a home in his mind also.

The sun was shining as the *Radgate* moved out of the dock and into the river. Mason, bare-headed, his shirt-sleeves rolled up, left Gates working on the starboard Oerlikon and went across to see how Rickman and the new boy, Braddock, were getting on with the port gun. The shore artificers had had this gun stripped down to see whether it had come to any harm from the fire, but they could discover nothing seriously wrong with it.

"All they did," Rickman said, "was make it a damn sight muckier that it was when they started on it. Artissifer — there's a cushy job if you like. Messing around all day with a bag of tools — no parades, no guard duty, plenty of pay. What more could you want?"

They had supplied a new cover and a

new bag for the empty cartridge-cases, and they had also replaced the rubber on the eyepiece and the shoulder-rests. Otherwise it was the same gun that Scarr had used. Mason hoped Braddock would have more luck with it.

He went down aft to have a word with the naval ratings and see that the twin Oerlikon was in order. He had no doubt that it would be.

Sims said: "I've got some copies of *New Writing* if you want something to read."

"Thanks," Mason said. He would have a look at them to please Sims, but *New Writing* did not really appeal to him — all those agonized souls being poured out in imitation Chekhov. He liked a story that was a story, with a beginning, a middle, and an end. These chunks of life might be art — Sims would have maintained stoutly that they were — but he preferred the work of Somerset Maugham, Kipling, de Maupassant, Damon Runyon, or even O. Henry. Sims had lent him a volume of short stories by Katherine Mansfield, and he had ploughed half-way through it before giving up in exasperation.

"I think she's a genius," Sims had said.

Mason thought Sims was deluding himself; but he was in good company.

Gates was checking ammunition when Mason returned to the bridge.

"I bought a balalaika in Archangel," Gates said. "That is, I exchanged a hundred fags for it. But I gave it to a cross-eyed carpenter."

"Why did you do that?"

"I couldn't play it."

"Could he?"

"No; but he thought he could. He'd got a tin ear."

"Nice for him," Mason said; and wondered what Jo was doing.

Off Southend they anchored and waited for the convoy. A naval craft brought them a balloon and transferred it to the *Radgate*'s masthead. A petty officer requested them in strong terms to bring it back in one piece.

"These things cost money."

"Hark at him," Gates said. "You'd think he paid for them hisself."

"Perhaps he does. Perhaps they dock the price out of his pay."

"He wouldn't get much if he did. He'd have to serve for the rest of his life to try and make it up."

The trip down-Channel was quiet. A Dutch motor-vessel chugged along on the port beam, sometimes gaining a little on the *Radgate*, sometimes dropping a little way astern. One or two high-powered naval launches thundered up and down the lines, and a Spitfire kept watch in the sky; but the escort was not conspicuous. This crocodile of ships was not like a deep-sea convoy that might be spread out over many square miles of ocean, with destroyers making a ring round it like cowboys circling a herd of cattle moving slowly across an endless prairie. Here the land was constantly visible, slipping past on the starboard side — glimpses of cliffs and beaches, green fields, church-towers, lighthouses, and clusters of buildings dipping down towards the sea like so much rubble tipped from a lorry down the sloping side of a pit. You were able to judge the progress of the ship by the changing contour of this land, but in mid-ocean you sailed for weeks and the only change was in the sea and the sky — and perhaps in the diminishing number of the ships.

This time they went straight to the beaches; there was no waiting in the Solent. In the brief interval since D-Day much had happened; most important of all, the Mulberry harbour of concrete caissons and scuttled ships was well on the way to completion — an engineering miracle that was taken for granted by those who used it.

"They've done some work since we were here last," Gates said. "Been at it like niggers."

It was like coming back to a house that you had left just emerging from its foundations; you looked to see how high the walls had grown during your absence; you took a kind of proprietorial interest in the work, as though this were something that was being done under your orders and your direction.

"Beached some of the coasters," Gates said. "That's not a bad idea."

There was a line of them, high and dry, looking as if they had been cast up by a spring tide and abandoned. It was low water, and the sand was hard enough for motor-trucks to drive alongside and take the cargo from them. Mason had not realized that ships could stand so firmly upright upon their keels with no more support than the slight channel in the sand made by their own weight. He hoped they would be able to float off again when the time came. Gates seemed to think this would be easy enough.

"When they're light they'll be able to claw off on the high tide."

"I hope you're right."

"Oh, no doubt about it."

There seemed to be more ocean-going cargo vessels at anchor than there had been when they had left. Many of these now had their names painted in big white letters along each side to make it easier to pick them out in the crowd. There were a number of Liberty ships — ships whose names began with Sam — ships with heavy-lift derricks that could draw a forty-ton tank out of the hold and swing it over the bulwarks into the tank-landing craft.

"Tricky work, that," Gates said. "Especially with a bit of a swell on. Knock a hole through the bottom of the barge before you know where you are. Tricky business altogether — landing tanks on beaches. Reminds me of when we were doing this sort of job in North Africa — a barge grounded on what they thought was the beach; turned out to be sandbank. When they let the ramp down and sent the first tank out it just disappeared in about two fathoms of water. One of the hazards of the game, of course, but what I say is, if you're going to do underwater stuff you might as well join the Submarine Service and have done with it."

They moved in slowly, cautiously, admonished by loud-hailers. It was like being conducted to a vacant space in a car-park, with a corvette or a launch in place of a white-coated attendant. When the anchor chain rattled out through the hawse-pipe, and the ship swung slowly round with the tide, there was a feeling almost of having returned home, a feeling of having come back after a brief holiday, even a spell of truancy.

Mason looked up at the balloon, floating silver-grey above the mast, and noted that already it was losing its gas, developing a certain flabbiness, like a man whose muscles have softened with age.

"We'll not be taking that one back," he said.

The sappers who came on board to do the unloading were strangers — not the ones who had gone out in the *Radgate* on D-Day. They said that ashore things were becoming organized. "Naafi stores coming in now — blanco and metal-polish first, naturally. The War's nearly won now."

They wanted to know all about the flying-bombs. They had heard garbled tales about the damage to London, and some of their homes were there.

"Is it right that half of it's been knocked for six?"

"Not yet," Mason said. "There seems to be plenty still standing."

"You loaded in London, did you?"

"We certainly did — East India dock."

"Well, if the docks are still working it can't be all that bad. You hear so many lies you don't know what is the truth."

"You needn't worry about London," Mason said. He hoped it was true. Jo was in London. She would be scared of the flying-bombs now that he was not there. He wished that he had been able to go back to her for one more night; he had not liked leaving her in the mood that she had been in. He wished the *Radgate* had not sailed so soon.

He watched the sappers working the winches, bringing the cargo up out of the hold. Each of these men must have his personal problems, his personal worries, just as he had his, but they were all involved in the one great problem that had to be solved before they would go back to living their own lives in their own ways. For the present they were cogs in a machine, and as the machine moved so must they move also, not independently but cohesively, each giving his effort in the common cause. The men who refused to give that effort, the men like Watts, were outcasts, hunted men, non-conformers.

The memory of Watts came unwelcome to Mason's mind. He wanted to forget Watts — if that were ever possible.

He saw that the first D.U.K.W. had been loaded and was heading away towards the shore. He watched it moving through the water, the gap between it and the ship gradually widening. He watched it until it came to the beach and became land-borne instead of water-borne, watched it, high on its four wheels, go off into the distance — inland. How far? How many miles inland had the perimeter of the bridge head been pushed?

Mason asked one of the sappers. The man shrugged. "Ten miles — maybe twenty. No far yet."

"It's a long way when you're fighting," Mason said.

"I suppose so. The Yanks are pushing ahead too. If they capture Cherbourg it'll make a difference."

"If Jerry hasn't made it unusable."

"Ah, he's likely to do that. Senseless bloody business all round when you come to think about it."

At night the artillery barrage was visible like a leaping flame along the skyline, the sound of it like the steady, distant rumble of thunder.

"Glad they aren't shooting at us," Gates said. "We must have put some guns ashore to make a show like that.

They'll need some ammo. Proper Brock's benefit."

Mason was glad to see and hear the barrage. Not until this moment had he felt convinced that the Allied armies were back in Europe to stay. There had always been the sneaking feeling that this might yet be working up to another defeat, another fiasco. Like a nagging voice at the back of his mind had always been the word Dieppe. Was this to be another Dieppe? Now, watching the guns reddening the night sky with their tongues of fire, he felt assured that there would be no retreat. Perhaps this time it would really be over by Christmas.

On the following day the *Radgate* drew up her anchor and moved in on the high tide until the sand grated under her keel. At low water the soil of France was visible on either side of the ship, and Army lorries, the damp sand clinging to their tyres, were being loaded from the derricks.

According to the cook, it was stark lunacy. "Here we are and here we'll stick."

"That's your opinion, is it?" Mason asked.

"Of course it's my opinion. If I was captain of a ship I'd never let its bottom touch solid ground except in dry-dock."

"You don't put much faith in Captain Garner, then?"

The cook was wary. "I never said that. I'm not saying anything against the master of this ship. He has his orders from higher authority. I have had hard words from Captain Garner, very hard words; but what of that? I'm saying nothing against him. But he's a man like other men. He walks on two legs, and he can't work miracles."

The cook opened the lid of the stove and spat into it with the accuracy of one who has had much practice. He rolled himself a cigarette and lit it from a shovelful of glowing coals that threatened to set his eyebrows on fire. With the cigarette adhering to his lower lip as though glued in position, he relieved his feelings by attacking a piece of dough on the cooking-board.

"You think we're going to have trouble, then?" Mason said.

"Trouble! What do I know about trouble? I'm just the cook. I'm just a one-eyed bastard that don't signify nothing. But" — he tapped Mason's chest with the end of a rolling-pin — "if you really ask my opinion, it's this: I'll be a whole lot easier in my mind when we're afloat again than what I am now. That's straight, isn't it? That's honest, isn't it? That's telling you, isn't it?"

"It is."

"So all right, then," the cook said. "Don't come to me afterwards and say I didn't warn you."

"I won't do that," Mason said. But he wondered exactly what it was that the cook was warning him about.

The cook worked away at his dough, rolling it out, folding it up, and then rolling it out again. He seemed to be using it simply as a means of giving exercise to his hand, with no other object in view. The dough had been made with that rare commodity, white flour, but it had acquired a greyish look, as though it had aged on the cooking-board and would never again know the joy, the hope, the abandon of youth.

The cook himself looked like that too. He had passed the point in life beyond which a man no longer has any hope of better things to come; his ambitions blunted by disappointment, he is resigned to a mediocre existence that will get no better and may well get worse. The cook was a pessimist, looking to the future without pleasurable expectation and gazing back at the past with a nostalgic longing for things that probably existed only in an imaginative memory. He rested his fingers in the dough and peered at Mason with his good eye, its glass partner apparently intent on something beyond the confines of the galley — perhaps a better world where cooks were appreciated at their true value.

"I remember," he said, "a favourite saying of Count Alberto — always expect the worst to happen because it surely will. It happened to him all right; he was shot by a servant girl who got a religious mania and thought he was Pontius Pilate." He rubbed his chin, leaving little blobs of dough distributed among the bristles. "The Count was right. I been in this world a matter of fifty-two years and I never found him wrong yet. That's why I'm expecting the worst to happen to this ship."

"You're a damned old Jeremiah," Mason said, and left him to brood on misfortune in solitude.

One of the steam winches appeared to have broken down, bringing the work of unloading the after hold to a standstill. Mason, in the course of his wandering about the ship, saw the chief engineer himself busy on it with spanner and screwdriver. Mr Mawby was sweating, the sappers were lounging about the deck, and at the side of the ship a lorry waited.

It was perhaps an unfortunate moment for the mate to put in an appearance, but, needing to move from the bridge to the poop, he could not avoid passing close by the sweating Mawby. All might have been well if he had been content simply to pass by, but some demon prompted him to make a remark, something that no man in the ordinary way could have taken exception to.

"Having a little trouble, Mr Mawby?"

The chief engineer was not a man in the ordinary way. To him the remark conveyed more than a friendly inquiry; it suggested criticism, scorn, an entire lack of belief in his engineering abilities, his qualifications, his fitness for the post he occupied. It was as though Gregory had said: 'Call yourself an engineer! You couldn't keep a toy train running. Personally, I wouldn't trust you to file a finger-nail, you incompetent booby.'

Mr Mawby dashed the sweat from his eyes and stood up, the spanner gripped in his right hand. "I'd be obliged," he said, "if you'd get to hell out of my way. When I'm doing a job of work I have a certain objection to damn fools peering over my shoulder and making damn-fool remarks. So if you don't move your carcase away from here, Mister Gregory, you may get a swipe with this spanner. I'm warning you."

The mate reddened. To be talked to in this manner before a gaping crowd of witnesses was not to his taste. It was injurious to his self-esteem. He could not leave matters at such a point and just walk away. He would have lost face; and

Mr Gregory was as much concerned with the preservation of face as any Oriental.

"Now, now," he said. "There's no need to be rude. Just because the job's a bit more than you can handle, you don't have to start throwing insults around."

Mr Mawby, heated already, seemed to hiss with steam. "More than I can handle, indeed! Why, you half-witted apology for a seaman, I could handle this job and punch your damned interfering snout at the same time. And, god-dammit, that's what I will do if you don't shift your fat arse in double quick time."

The mate planted his feet wide and stood his ground. He was breathing heavily with anger. "You'll apologize for those words. You'll apologize here and now before I move an inch."

Mr Mawby's steam came to a head quite suddenly and blew the safety-valve. Like a man cracking the shell of an egg with a spoon, he lifted the spanner and tapped Mr Gregory on the head. Mr Gregory sat down on the deck, yelling blue murder, and Mr Mawby, having satisfactorily attended to one task, returned with an admirable display of placidity to the other.

★ ★ ★

"It's an omen," the cook said, ladling out dry hash for tea. "It's an omen of worse to come."

Mason looked at the mess on his plate. "Impossible," he said. "There just couldn't be anything worse than this — not without being downright uneatable."

The cook looked pained. "Allow me to inform you," he said, in a stiff, dignified voice that scarcely matched his general ruffianly appearance, "that this is as good a specimen of dry hash as you'd be likely to find if you was to search the length and breadth of the globe." He tapped Mason's chest with a dirty forefinger tipped by a blackened nail. "Epicures have complimented me on my skill in the preparation of that dish — epicures. Signor Martinelli of Martinelli's restaurant — which you, being an educated man, have no doubt heard of — Signor M himself once said to me, 'My boy, if there is anyone else in the world who can make dry hash as good as what you do, I have yet to find him.'"

"He called you 'My boy,' did he?"

"I was younger in them days," the cook said.

"All the same, I don't see what that's got to do with omens."

"I was not referring to food when I made that remark. I was thinking about this little set-to between the mate and the chief. The mate swears he'll sue Mawby for damages when we get back to England. Maybe he will, too; he took a nasty crack on the bean. But that sort of thing's bad in a ship — real bad. That's why I say it's an omen."

"You've got omens on the brain," Mason said. "The mate and the chief have been at loggerhead all along. Just because it's come to blows doesn't mean the ship is going to fall apart."

"There's such things as bombs, ain't there?"

"Certainly. But I don't think we're going to get any. I haven't seen any Jerry planes about this trip."

"There's mines."

"There's old age, too," Mason said. "That's what I intend to die of."

"You may be lucky."

The cook was gloomy, but there was nothing in the weather to relieve his gloom. Looking seaward, Mason could see white caps on the waves. The ships at anchor were stirring uneasily, tugging at their cables as if to test the strength of those iron hooks that held them fastened to the bottom of the sea. Above the *Radgate*'s mast the flabby balloon danced in the wind. It was a cold wind, coming from the north-east, and it seemed to be growing stronger. Mason saw Captain Garner come out on to the bridge and look towards the sea — the sea that was coming in with a line of white foam and creeping up the sides of the ship.

"The Old Man's worried. Maybe we're in for a gale. That'd be handy."

It was Gates, who had come out of the forecastle to stand beside Mason — Gates scratching his chest and looking wise. "Get a nice gale now and what's going to happen to the unloading schedule?

This lark's all very well in calm weather, but not so good if it turns nasty. What are you going to do about that balloon, sarge?"

"To hell with the balloon. There's nothing we can do. What it needs is a shot of gas, but it won't get it. If it comes down it comes down, and that's all there is to it. Just too bad."

He refused to worry his head about balloons. They were expendable.

He looked away from the sea and over the shattered concrete and torn barbed wire along the shore. He looked inland, listening to the rumble of the guns. Men were expendable too.

13

Storm

MASON was asleep in Gates's bunk when the real trouble started. Something — perhaps a heavier wave than usual beating against the hull — woke him. For a moment he lay there, staring up at the iron above him and listening to the wind, the creaking of the ship, and the splash of water.

It had been a wild enough night when he had come down off watch; now, at two o'clock in the morning, it seemed to have become even wilder. The ship was stirring uneasily, as though, with its keel still aground, it were being swayed from side to side, rocking in its groove.

It was not like the ordinary rolling of a ship at sea; it was jerkier, it was as though the vessel were a toy and some child were shaking it. Gates's towel, hanging on a cord between the bunk and the deckhead light to act as a curtain, was swinging like a pendulum. The oilskins hanging on the door of the cabin rustled as though they were alive, and simply awaiting the order to lift themselves off the hook and go tramping out into the night to deal with whatever emergency might have arisen. The lower door of the stove that until this moment had remained open fell shut with a clang and woke Rickman. Mason could hear him stirring in the lower bunk and muttering to himself.

It was no use trying to sleep again. Mason reached for a cigarette and lit it. He heard Rickman's voice, sounding just a little scared. "That you awake, sarge? What's happening?"

"We're taking a bit of a hammering, that's all." He leaned over the edge of the bunk and offered Rickman a cigarette. "Here, have a smoke. Unless you feel like going to sleep again."

Rickman took the cigarette. "Sleep! You'd need to be dead to sleep through this racket."

The movement and the din were certainly becoming more than it was possible to dismiss with a quip. There was something frightening about the way the ship quivered and groaned. Mason decided to get dressed. He pushed the blankets back and had one leg over the edge of the bunk and on the rail of the lower one just as the ship gave another violent lurch to port. Mason lost his grip and was flung across the cabin, coming to a halt with his back hard up against the door and his knees touching his chin.

"You all right?" Rickman asked anxiously.

"Depends what you mean by all right. I'm in one piece — I think."

The oilskins were draped round his head, and he could smell the sharp tang of them. He got up, feeling sore. The ship had returned to an even keel; and that was another queer thing — after rolling to port she did not then roll an equal distance to starboard; she simply staggered to the vertical position, with a kind of jerk and shudder that seemed to indicate that the effort was almost beyond her strength. And then she would wait for the next blow to lay her over to port. Mason suspected that she was no longer in her former position with her bows pointing inland, but that she had swung round until she was broadside on to the beach, in which position she was being pounded by the incoming waves.

"I'm going to have a look outside," he said.

He found his trousers and began to put them on, leaning back against the door in readiness for another lurch of the ship. It did not come at once, and Mason was able to button the trousers and fastened a webbing belt about his waist without difficulty.

"You think something's wrong?" Rickman asked.

"What should be wrong?"

"I don't know. But I was talking to the cook, and he said — "

"Oh, so you've been talking to him to. Well, you don't have to take too much notice of that joker. He's a cast-iron pessimist. I think he enjoys looking on the black side of things."

He began to pull on his gumboots, tucking the trousers into them.

"All the same — " Rickman began. But he never finished what he was going to say, for at that precise moment the steel plates of the bows alongside which Rickman's bunk was fixed suddenly bulged inward, the porthole burst open with a shatter of glass, and a gush of sea-water jetted into the cabin.

Several things recorded themselves on Mason's senses all at once — a shrieking, grinding noise of metal on metal, a scream of pain from Rickman that ended abruptly as if it had been smothered, a wedge of steel poking through the torn side of the cabin like the point of an immense tinopener, a kaleidoscope of lights flashing across his eyes as the cabin floor rose under his feet and flung him violently against the stove; and then darkness and the feel of water and the sound of water and the grinding of the wedge as it shifted in the gap it had torn.

He rolled away from the stove and tried to stand up in the darkness, but the floor was tilted at a sharp angle, and all kinds of things seemed to have fallen on to it. Then he felt the unmistakable touch of oilskins under his hand, and knew that he must be close to the door. The water was still coming in,

339

he could hear it; it made a sound like that of a fire-hydrant turned full on — a frightening, threatening sound, the sound of death in a ship. The water was swirling round Mason's legs, hampering his movement as he pulled himself up by the door; already some of it had trickled into his gumboots. It felt very cold, with the coldness of death.

He was worried about Rickman. Things had moved so quickly that he had not been able to see what had happened to the boy. There had been the one brief, agonized scream, then silence.

He called: "Rick! Rick! Are you all right?" But there was no answer except the steady gush of water and the groaning of metal.

Mason groped in his hip-pocket for his petrol-lighter, found it and pulled it out. He flicked it, and for a moment was afraid that his lighter that had never yet let him down was going to do so now; but at the third attempt it burst into flame, a yellow, flickering light that showed as a series of shadows the chaos around him. The water was not coming in quite so fast now, but the floor was still tilted to port, and in the trough formed along the line of the bulkhead in which the door was situated the water had collected. The packing-case that was used as a table was half afloat, and a life-jacket that had been flung down in one corner rested upon the surface of the water like a dead bird, surrounded by the smaller flotsam of match-stalks and bits of paper. There was froth on the water like the head on a mug of beer, but it had a dark, sinister appearance that might have been partly due to the poor illumination.

Mason called again, "Rick! Rick!" and then stopped calling, seeing the futility of ever calling to Rickman again.

The two bunks had been twisted into a strange, tortured shape like the frame of a motor-cycle that has been involved in a collision. Rickman, lying in the lower one, had been caught between the thrust-in side of the ship and the iron rail of the bunk as though in the jaws of a giant mousetrap. In that trap he had been crushed with savage force. The rail had gone into his body, and there he hung with his broken limbs, draped over it as gamekeepers hang dead vermin on a wire fence. By some freak of circumstance the rail had thrust itself into his mouth like a bit, so that it seemed as though he were trying to bite through that tube of metal. But he was dead, and the water pouring in upon him carried his blood away in a crimson stream.

Mason saw at a glance that he could give no help to Rickman, that the boy was beyond help in this world. He realized too that if he did not quickly get out of the flooding cabin he might himself soon be as dead as Rickman. He turned away from the grim, reminder of mortality in the bunk and went splashing back down the slope of the cabin to the door. He gripped the handle with his right hand and tried to pull the door open, but it did not budge. He extinguished the lighter and put it back in his pocket. Then he tried with both hands to open the door. He could make no impression on it. Either it had become jammed at the moment when the ship was rammed or the weight of water was holding it shut.

Terror flickered up in Mason. In the darkness, with the sound of the water pouring in behind him, carrying with it Rickman's blood, he clawed frenziedly at the door-handle, yelling for help. This frenzy lasted for perhaps thirty seconds; then he took a grip on himself. He thought: I must not panic; I must think, think. There must be some way out.

He remembered that the door was not particularly strong. He might be able to break out one of the panels if he could find some implement. If only he had an axe! But there was no axe in the cabin. The irony of it was that in the alleyway there was a small chopper hanging beside two fire-buckets. If he had been on the other side of the door he could have broken it down. But if he had been on the other side of the door he would have had no need to do so.

The water had risen above his knees, and his boots were filled; yet in spite of its coldness he felt hot. He felt as though he could not breathe in the cabin, as though the air were pressing upon him like cotton-wool. He put a hand in the water and dashed some of it into his face. He tasted the salt, and then he remembered how Rickman's blood had poured into that water, mingling its crimson river with the salt, and he was suddenly and violently sick. He thought he could hear his vomit splashing in the water at his feet, but it might have been the stream that was still flowing through the rent side. The ship gave another lurch, staggering under another blow, and in the darkness behind Mason the iron creaked.

He remembered that there used to be an iron marline-spike lying by the stove. Gates had told him that it was used as a poker when the fire was alight. He groped his way up the slope of the floor until his hands touched the stove, and then he began searching for the spike with his fingers. The water was shallower here, but nevertheless his face was close to it, and the thought of Rickman's blood plagued him.

After a time he gave up searching for the spike and stood up. He stretched out a hand to steady himself, and the hand touched a man's face — Rickman's face, with the rail imbedded in it. He drew his hand away with a shudder, and went slipping back down the slope to the door.

He set his foot on something that rolled away from under him, and he fell backward into the water. But he guessed that the rolling thing he had stood on must be the marline-spike. He had to put his head under the water to find it, and he came up gasping and dripping, his hair down over his eyes and his shirt clinging like a wet dishcloth. But he had the spike.

Now he had lost the door. In the thick darkness he could not recall in which direction he had to move; his brain seemed to have become clogged, to have stopped working. He stood for what seemed like a full minute, listening to the inflow of water, and the groaning of the ship, before his brain clicked into action once again and he realized that he simply had to move down the slope and feel along the bulkhead for the door.

"You're a fool, Peter Mason," he said aloud, taking courage from the sound of his own voice. "Don't panic now. Just take things calmly and everything will be all right — all right."

He would have been glad of some light, but he knew that his petrol-lighter would be soaked by now, and that it would have been a waste of time to try it. He licked his lips, and tasted the salt and the slime on them. He spat out the saliva from his mouth and moved down the slope.

He found the oilskins almost at once, and wrenched them from the hook. Then he lifted the marline-spike in both hands and plunged it into the door. The wood was tougher than he had expected; the point of the spike went into it, but not through. It jarred his hands, and the shock went up through his arms and into his head. When he struck again he could not be sure of hitting the same place; it was like hitting, blindfold, at a punch-bag. He struck again and again, with no more apparent effect than if he had been striking at the trunk of a tree.

The water had crept up to his waist. He could feel the circle of it about his stomach like the grip of an icy belt. It seemed to be paralysing the lower half of his body. He felt as in a nightmare, held by the water and striking again and again at the door he could not see, unable to tell whether he were making an impression or not.

Then, as though some pressure had been momentarily eased, the ship moved back on to a more even keel. It did not become quite upright, but the list to port became less acute. Mason could feel the water flowing away from the door, falling to the level of his knees. He tensed his muscles and lunged into the darkness with the marline-spike. He heard the wood splinter, and knew that the spike had penetrated. He levered it from side to side, enlarging the hole; then, working by touch, began chipping away at the splintered wood.

Now that he had succeeded in making the first small hole his confidence returned. In a few moment he was able to push his hand through the door, and he could feel the fresher air that flowed into the cabin. He redoubled his efforts, and the wood, having at last begun to give way, made less resistance. Soon he judged that he had made a space large enough to crawl through. He put his head and shoulders through the gap, and managed to get a grip on a hand-rail in the alleyway. His gumboots were impeding him, so he kicked them off. Then with the aid of the rail, he gave a final heave and came out of the hole like a cork coming out of a bottle.

For a while he lay where he had fallen in the alleyway with water swilling round him; then he got up and stumbled out of the forecastle on to the open deck.

As he emerged from the doorway he caught a glimpse of something glimmering whitely in the darkness to his left — something that came sweeping towards him. He tried to dodge it, but was too late. The wave came over the side of the *Radgate* and thundered down on the foredeck. It caught Mason in its grip and flung him hard against the coaming of the hatch. He felt as if the life were being jarred out of him, as if his body were nothing but a rag doll to be broken helplessly on the iron of the hatch, as if all the seas of the world were crashing down on him, beating him to pulp.

But when the water had left him, swilling away towards the scuppers, he found, somewhat to his surprise, that he was still able to move and to stand up.

Out here in the open there was not that

total darkness that had oppressed him in the cabin. Indeed, he was able to see the outlines of the hatch-cover, the winches, the derricks, and the bridge — all like shadows, but unmistakable. The noise was incessant: the wind buffeting in from the sea roused a howl of protest from every shroud and halyard, every piece of loose canvas and every wire-rope and ventilator shaft; the howl varied in pitch and volume, but never died completely away; and as the ground-bass to this tune there was the constant thunder of waves breaking on the ship and on the beach. There might also have been the shouts of men, but Mason could not tell, for the human voice would have been powerless to carry more than a few yards in such a boisterous night. What he did hear as the ship moved was the sound of cargo shifting in the hold, and he wondered how much movement of that kind would be needed to spark off an explosion that would blow the whole ship to pieces.

As he struggled to his feet, bracing himself against the wind, he saw beyond the starboard bulwark a dark mass like a great rock moving through the night.

It was not distinguishable as a ship, but there was nothing else it could be. It seemed to rear up suddenly like a black monster over-topping the *Radgate*, to bear down on her and crash into her side with just such a groaning, tearing, cracking noise as Mason had heard when the forecastle cabin had been crushed in and poor Rickman had been killed. The *Radgate* reeled under the blow, lay over on her port side, and Mason was flung sprawling on the hatch-cover.

The idea came to him in a vague mass of ideas that he must get to the bridge. He did not know what he could do when he got there, but he felt that the bridge was the nerve-centre of the ship, and that there was his action station.

He found the first ladder, and it was leaning over at such an acute angle that he had to grip the starboard hand-rail with both hands and half drag himself up. The second ladder was the same, but he managed both climbs, feeling the ribbing on the steps through the thickness of his socks. He was glad to see Gates, for he had not encounterd a human being since his escape from the cabin, and the last face he had seen had been the dead face of Rickman, with the iron bar in its mouth.

Gates shouted: "That you, sarge? Here's a fine to-do and no mistake."

Mason hung on to the side of the gun-box, panting. "What in hell's been happening?"

"Hell's right." Gates pointed into the confusion of darkness beyond the starboard side. "That ship. Must be out of control. Rammed us twice already. God knows what damage it'll do before it's finished. We'll be over on our side before long."

"It's done some damage already. Smashed a hole in the cabin. Killed Rickman."

"Rickie — dead?" Gates seemed unable to believe it. "Rickie — dead? How?"

"Hell; does it matter how? Crushed, mangled, smashed; d'you understand?" He remembered Rickman's face, remembered putting his hand on that face in the darkness. His body shook with a sudden reaction, delayed until this moment. "We'll be lucky if we're not soon all dead. Lucky if the cargo doesn't blow us all to hell."

He was aware then that a third figure was standing on the wing of the bridge — a thick, stocky figure. He heard Captain Garner's voice grinding its way out of that figure.

"What's that you say about the cargo?"

"It's shifting," Mason said. "Rolling a t all over the place. And there's a hole in the bows. And Rickman's been killed."

He was thinking: This man should do something. He's the captain; it's his job to take things in hand before worse happens.

He did not pause to consider how things could be taken in hand. It was not his job. But something ought to be done. It was no use just standing there and waiting for the ship to blow up.

* * *

Captain Garner began to speak again, but before he could utter two words something whipped out of the darkness like a snake and caught him by the throat. It dragged him choking, back against the wheel house with a twang like the plucked string of a guitar. Garner's heels beat madly on the woodwork, his hands clawed at the wire about his throat. It tightened remorselessly, cutting through flesh and sinew until his head was half-severed from his body and there was no more life in him.

A shape like a great white bird went flapping across the ship and fell into the water. The wire loosened, and Garner slid down the side of the wheelhouse like heap of old clothes.

"The balloon!" Mason shouted. "The balloon!"

The balloon had come down like a shot bird, dragging its wire across the bridge, and catching Garner in the loop. The wind had blown and the wire had drawn tight and Garner was dead — dead as Rickman in his bunk, dead as the airman plunging earthward in the burning remnants of his plane, dead as the child buried in the ruin of the bombed house.

Mason went down on his knees beside Garner, but even in the darkness it was plain that Garner stood in no need of his help, that he would never again need help from any human hand. His head lolled away from his body like the head of a puppet, and the blood was gushing out.

Mason stood up and yelled for Gates, trying to make his voice heard above the shrieking of the wind. "Where's the mate? Have you seen him?"

"He was on the bridge ten minutes ago."

"I'm going to find him."

He turned towards the wheel house, and almost fell over Garner's dog. The animal was whimpering; it went to the body and began to nuzzle it, whining and whimpering all the time.

Mason went into the wheelhouse, shouting: "Mr Gregory! Mr Gregory!" There was no answer. He went out on to the other side of the bridge, and came upon Gunner Braddock.

Braddock said: "The mate went down aft." Braddock was scared. His voice trembled. Mason could understand how he felt, with the ship half over on its side and the seas pounding it and the wind wailing. But he had no time to try reassuring Braddock. He went to the ladder, and as he began to descend he could hear the dog howling.

He was half-way down the ladder when the ship received its final blow; he never knew whether it came from the other ship or merely from the sea. It made no difference whence the blow came; it was effective, it rolled the *Radgate* over on to its beam-ends, and there was no coming up again.

Mason grabbed at the rail, felt his arm jerked savagely back, felt a blow on his knee, and knew that he was falling helplessly. He hit the water with a smack that drove the wind out of his body. He took a mouthful of brine and went under. When he came to the surface he found that he had no power in his right arm; it moved as the water took it, like something loosely attached but not really belonging to him. When it moved it sent flashes of pain searing through his shoulder; and he could not prevent it from moving.

A wave lifted him and carried him forward, and something lashed at his legs — a rope or some part of the ship's rigging. Now and then he caught a glimpse of the dark shape of the *Radgate* behind and above him, and he was fearful that it might be lifted by the sea and flung down on top of him. Faintly he could hear men shouting, but they seemed a very long way away; he had a feeling of being cut off from them, to have no more to do with the crew of that ship.

He knew that he had to get to the beach; it was on the beach that his chance of survival depended. He began to struggle forward, using his left arm and his legs, but his clothing hampered him and he could not tell whether he was making any headway. The waves seemed to draw him back as much as they sent him forward, so that he was like a shuttle, moving first one way and then the other, getting nowhere.

Suddenly his left hand made contact with something hard and unyielding, half submerged in the water. He tried to grasp it, not realizing at first that it was the top of one of *Radgate*'s masts. Then he felt the pulley through which the balloon cable was rove, and then the wire itself, and he let go and kicked himself away for fear that he should become entangled in that deadly wire. At that moment he bumped into another man, and the man grabbed at his broken right arm, so that with the pain he yelled in agony: "Let go. Let go, damn you!"

The man let go and shouted: "Whos' that? Who's that?"

Mason recognized the cook's voice, but another wave carried the cook away from him, and he struck out again with his legs and his one good arm and felt as though now he were being carried shoreward on the crest. And in fact in a moment later he could feel the sand under his feet. He fell forward on his face and the wave crashed down on him, trying to drag him back again with the undertow. But he dug his feet and his fingers in and crawled forward — up out of the sea. He had gone out of France four years before, a fugitive from the beaches of Dunkirk; now he had come back to the beaches of Arromanches like a castaway washed up by the tide, with a broken arm and a half-drowned body.

And as he lay on the sand, waiting for the strength to come back to his body, he saw a flash of light and heard an explosion, and had time to think. The ship's blown up! Before the piece of metal struck the back of his head and thrust him into the black pit of unconsciousness.

14

Ruins

MASON came out of hospital in November. It seemed to him that so long a time had passed since he had been wounded that the whole world must have altered. In a way it had, for with the Allied armies moving in strength across the ruined face of Europe it could now be only a matter of a few months before they linked up with the Russians advancing from the east and finished off the last desperate German resistance.

Gates had been to see Mason, had sat by his bedside and given him the news. He had told him about the cook, that moody singer and concoctor of weird dishes, that pessimist always expecting the worst to happen, and seldom disappointed.

"Must have crawled out of the water just after you by all accounts. Stood on one of those anti-personnel mines what the sappers had overlooked — careless shower."

"Poor old cook," Mason said. "No more songs from him; no more dry hash. I thought it was the ship going up."

"You wouldn't be here now if it had been."

"True enough."

In fact the *Radgate*'s cargo had been practically all salvaged — though some of it was in a useless condition. The ship itself, like many others caught by that six-day June storm, had been a total loss. The storm had broken the Mulberry harbour on the American beach, but the British one had stood firm even against that onslaught, and the landing of supplies had gone on. Two men of the *Radgate*'s crew had been drowned in trying to get ashore; four others had been injured; but the rest had escaped with nothing more serious than bruises and sprains.

"What happened to the dog?" Mason asked.

"Cerberus is all right. The mate took him."

Gates was wearing sergeant's stripes — new stripes on a brand-new battle-dress. "They pushed me up again," he explained. "Must be short of sergeants." He lowered his voice so that the nurse should not hear him. "The fact is I've been warned for embarkation with a Bofors team. The sweet run. Russia."

"It's quieter up there now."

"It may be quiet and it may be not. But it'll be cold; either way it'll be filthy cold."

"You've got plenty of fat. You won't notice."

Mason was sorry to hear that Gates was going. He had thought of confiding in Gates about Jo. Perhaps Gates would go and see her, tell her that he was alive, that he had not forgotten. But if Gates was off to Russia there would be no time for that.

"Give my love to Uncle Joe," he said.

★ ★ ★

Clare came to see him too as soon as they would allow her to do so. He felt uneasy

361

with her sitting beside the bed, looking cool and beautiful and concerned. He felt as though he were deceiving her.

And yet he liked having Clare there, and was sorry when she had to go. He would have liked to have told her about Jo. Perhaps she would have understood. But it would have hurt her; and he did not wish to hurt Clare.

★ ★ ★

Going back into the remembered streets was like going back into a past life. Time had thrown up a barrier. He could not recall exactly what Jo looked like, could not recall her face or her voice. They had become blurred — as a face seen through misted glass, as a voice heard far off. If he were to meet her now suddenly in the street he felt that he would need to look twice to be sure that it was she. For a few days they had been so close to one another; now they would be as strangers meeting. But the strangeness would pass — quickly.

When he came to where the house had stood he did not at first believe what his eyes told him. Surely he must have come to the wrong street? But when he had checked up he knew that this was the place — this expanse of rubble and mortar and broken beams. And he knew too that the destruction had not been recent; time had weathered the ruins, blunting the jagged edges. Perhaps this thing had happened on the very day when he had left her . Perhaps she had still been there, lying with her head buried in the pillow, when the bomb had fallen. He supposed that it had been a V1, not an ordinary bomb. Yet what did it matter? The result was the same either way.

He grasped at hope. Perhaps she had not been in the house. How could he tell? The bomb might have fallen when she was at work, out shopping, anywhere.

Even when he had read the name on a list he still could not at first accept the fact that she was dead. Josephine Carole Jackson — the name was strange to him; it did not bring a picture of Jo. Perhaps this was someone else; perhaps somewhere Jo was still alive. He would not believe that she was dead.

But he knew that he was deluding

himself. He knew that the incident was complete, finished, with the cruel, bitter finality of death.

He went back to the ruins, walking slowly, his feet dragging. He stood for a long time just staring at the place where the house had been. So this was what it came to in the end, the gaiety, the laughter, the tears — a few broken timbers, some smoke-blackened rubble, dust.

A boy came and stared up into his face with the unabashed curiosity of childhood. He had a snub nose and a rash of freckles; his hair made a straight fringe across his forehead. Mason found a shilling in his pocket and dropped it into the boy's ready hand.

"Buy yourself the world."

The boy said: "I'm going to be a Commando when I grow up. I'm going to have a Sten-gun and kill a million Germans."

"You're too late," Mason said. "Too damn late."

He lit a cigarette and tossed the dead match into the ruins of the house. Then he turned and walked away up the street.

Other titles in the
Ulverscroft Large Print Series:

TO FIGHT THE WILD
Rod Ansell and Rachel Percy

Lost in uncharted Australian bush, Rod Ansell survived by hunting and trapping wild animals, improvising shelter and using all the bushman's skills he knew.

COROMANDEL
Pat Barr

India in the 1830s is a hot, uncomfortable place, where the East India Company still rules. Amelia and her new husband find themselves caught up in the animosities which seethe between the old order and the new.

THE SMALL PARTY
Lillian Beckwith

A frightening journey to safety begins for Ruth and her small party as their island is caught up in the dangers of armed insurrection.

CLOUD OVER MALVERTON
Nancy Buckingham

Dulcie soon realises that something is seriously wrong at Malverton, and when violence strikes she is horrified to find herself under suspicion of murder.

AFTER THOUGHTS
Max Bygraves

The Cockney entertainer tells stories of his East End childhood, of his RAF days, and his post-war showbusiness successes and friendships with fellow comedians.

MOONLIGHT
AND MARCH ROSES
D. Y. Cameron

Lynn's search to trace a missing girl takes her to Spain, where she meets Clive Hendon. While untangling the situation, she untangles her emotions and decides on her own future.

NURSE ALICE IN LOVE
Theresa Charles

Accepting the post of nurse to little Fernie Sherrod, Alice Everton could not guess at the romance, suspense and danger which lay ahead at the Sherrod's isolated estate.

POIROT INVESTIGATES
Agatha Christie

Two things bind these eleven stories together — the brilliance and uncanny skill of the diminutive Belgian detective, and the stupidity of his Watson-like partner, Captain Hastings.

LET LOOSE THE TIGERS
Josephine Cox

Queenie promised to find the long-lost son of the frail, elderly murderess, Hannah Jason. But her enquiries threatened to unlock the cage where crucial secrets had long been held captive.

THE TWILIGHT MAN
Frank Gruber

Jim Rand lives alone in the California desert awaiting death. Into his hermit existence comes a teenage girl who blows both his past and his brief future wide open.

DOG IN THE DARK
Gerald Hammond

Jim Cunningham breeds and trains gun dogs, and his antagonism towards the devotees of show spaniels earns him many enemies. So when one of them is found murdered, the police are on his doorstep within hours.

THE RED KNIGHT
Geoffrey Moxon

When he finds himself a pawn on the chessboard of international espionage with his family in constant danger, Guy Trent becomes embroiled in moves and countermoves which may mean life or death for Western scientists.

TIGER TIGER
Frank Ryan

A young man involved in drugs is found murdered. This is the first event which will draw Detective Inspector Sandy Woodings into a whirlpool of murder and deceit.

CAROLINE MINUSCULE
Andrew Taylor

Caroline Minuscule, a medieval script, is the first clue to the whereabouts of a cache of diamonds. The search becomes a deadly kind of fairy story in which several murders have an other-worldly quality.

LONG CHAIN OF DEATH
Sarah Wolf

During the Second World War four American teenagers from the same town join the Army together. Forty-two years later, the son of one of the soldiers realises that someone is systematically wiping out the families of the four men.

THE LISTERDALE MYSTERY
Agatha Christie

Twelve short stories ranging from the light-hearted to the macabre, diverse mysteries ingeniously and plausibly contrived and convincingly unravelled.

TO BE LOVED
Lynne Collins

Andrew married the woman he had always loved despite the knowledge that Sarah married him for reasons of her own. So much heartache could have been avoided if only he had known how vital it was to be loved.

ACCUSED NURSE
Jane Converse

Paula found herself accused of a crime which could cost her her job, her nurse's reputation, and even the man she loved, unless the truth came to light.

A GREAT DELIVERANCE
Elizabeth George

Into the web of old houses and secrets of Keldale Valley comes Scotland Yard Inspector Thomas Lynley and his assistant to solve a particularly savage murder.

'E' IS FOR EVIDENCE
Sue Grafton

Kinsey Millhone was bogged down on a warehouse fire claim. It came as something of a shock when she was accused of being on the take. She'd been set up. Now she had a new client — herself.

A FAMILY OUTING IN AFRICA
Charles Hampton and Janie Hampton

A tale of a young family's journey through Central Africa by bus, train, river boat, lorry, wooden bicycle and foot.

THE PLEASURES OF AGE
Robert Morley

The author, British stage and screen star, now eighty, is enjoying the pleasures of age. He has drawn on his experiences to write this witty, entertaining and informative book.

THE VINEGAR SEED
Maureen Peters

The first book in a trilogy which follows the exploits of two sisters who leave Ireland in 1861 to seek their fortune in England.

A VERY PAROCHIAL MURDER
John Wainwright

A mugging in the genteel seaside town turned to murder when the victim died. Then the body of a young tearaway is washed ashore and Detective Inspector Lyle is determined that a second killing will not go unpunished.

DEATH ON A HOT SUMMER NIGHT
Anne Infante

Micky Douglas is either accident-prone or someone is trying to kill him. He finds himself caught in a desperate race to save his ex-wife and others from a ruthless gang.

HOLD DOWN A SHADOW
Geoffrey Jenkins

Maluti Rider, with the help of four of the world's most wanted men, is determined to destroy the Katse Dam and release a killer flood.

THAT NICE MISS SMITH
Nigel Morland

A reconstruction and reassessment of the trial in 1857 of Madeleine Smith, who was acquitted by a verdict of Not Proven of poisoning her lover, Emile L'Angelier.

SEASONS OF MY LIFE
Hannah Hauxwell
and Barry Cockcroft

The story of Hannah Hauxwell's struggle to survive on a desolate farm in the Yorkshire Dales with little money, no electricity and no running water.

TAKING OVER
Shirley Lowe and Angela Ince

A witty insight into what happens when women take over in the boardroom and their husbands take over chores, children and chickenpox.

AFTER MIDNIGHT STORIES,
The Fourth Book Of

A collection of sixteen of the best of today's ghost stories, all different in style and approach but all combining to give the reader that special midnight shiver.

DEATH TRAIN
Robert Byrne

The tale of a freight train out of control and leaking a paralytic nerve gas that turns America's West into a scene of chemical catastrophe in which whole towns are rendered helpless.

THE ADVENTURE OF THE CHRISTMAS PUDDING
Agatha Christie

In the introduction to this short story collection the author wrote "This book of Christmas fare may be described as 'The Chef's Selection'. I am the Chef!"

RETURN TO BALANDRA
Grace Driver

Returning to her Caribbean island home, Suzanne looks forward to being with her parents again, but most of all she longs to see Wim van Branden, a coffee planter she has known all her life.

SKINWALKERS
Tony Hillerman

The peace of the land between the sacred mountains is shattered by three murders. Is a 'skinwalker', one who has rejected the harmony of the Navajo way, the murderer?

A PARTICULAR PLACE
Mary Hocking

How is Michael Hoath, newly arrived vicar of St. Hilary's, to meet the demands of his flock and his strained marriage? Further complications follow when he falls hopelessly in love with a married parishioner.

A MATTER OF MISCHIEF
Evelyn Hood

A saga of the weaving folk in 18th century Scotland. Physician Gavin Knox was desperately seeking a cure for the pox that ravaged the slums of Glasgow and Paisley, but his adored wife, Margaret, stood in the way.

DEAD SPIT
Janet Edmonds

Government vet Linus Rintoul attempts to solve a mystery which plunges him into the esoteric world of pedigree dogs, murder and terrorism, and Crufts Dog Show proves to be far more exciting than he had bargained for . . .

A BARROW IN THE BROADWAY
Pamela Evans

Adopted by the Gordillo family, Rosie Goodson watched their business grow from a street barrow to a chain of supermarkets. But passion, bitterness and her unhappy marriage aliented her from them.

THE GOLD AND THE DROSS
Eleanor Farnes

Lorna found it hard to make ends meet for herself and her mother and then by chance she met two men — one a famous author and one a rich banker. But could she really expect to be happy with either man?

THE SONG OF THE PINES
Christina Green

Taken to a Greek island as substitute for David Nicholas's secretary, Annie quickly falls prey to the island's charms and to the charms of both Marcus, the Greek, and David himself.

GOODBYE DOCTOR GARLAND
Marjorie Harte

The story of a woman doctor who gave too much to her profession and almost lost her personal happiness.

DIGBY
Pamela Hill

Welcomed at courts throughout Europe, Kenelm Digby was the particular favourite of the Queen of France, who wanted him to be her lover, but the beautiful Venetia was the mainspring of his life.

**Books are to be returned on or before
the last date below.**

125
49
196
184